STUART McHARDY is a
musician, broadcaster
history and folklore. Since graduating with a
history degree from Edinburgh University in the
1970s he has found ongoing inspiration and
stimulus in our dynamic story and music traditions.
His research has led him far beyond his native
Scotland and he has lectured and performed in
many different parts of the world. Whether telling
stories to children or lecturing to adults, Stuart's
enthusiasm and love of his material make him an
entertaining and stimulating speaker.

His own enthusiasm and commitment have led
to him re-interpreting much of the history,
mythology and legends of Early Western Europe.
Combining the roles of scholar and performer gives
McHardy an unusually clear insight into tradition
and he sees connections and continuities that others
may have missed. As happy singing an old ballad as
analysing ancient legends he has held such diverse
positions as Director of the Scots Language
Resource Centre and President of the Pictish Arts
Society. He lives in Edinburgh with the lovely
Sandra and they have one son, Roderick. More
information about Stuart can be found at
www.wittins.demon.co.uk

By the same author

Luath Storyteller Series
Tales of Edinburgh Castle

STUART McHARDY

Luath Press Limited

EDINBURGH

www.luath.co.uk

First Published 2007
This Edition 2016

ISBN: 978-1-910021-76-7

The paper used in this book is acid-free, neutral-sized
and recyclable. It is made from low chlorine pulps
produced in a low energy, low emission manner from
renewable forests.

Printed and bound by
CPI Antony Rowe, Chippenham

Typeset in 10.5 point Sabon by
3btype.com

contents

Contents

Introduction

HISTORY IS ONLY ONE of the ways in which we try to understand the past. Tales, legends and mythology preserve ideas of how the world was in former times. Stories can last incredible lengths of time, recent research showing that some oral traditions have passed on verifiable information for tens of thousands of years. While such information might not fit the historian's wish for precise dates, times and locations, it can still tell us a lot about the past. With its magnificent outlook over the Firth of Forth, Edinburgh's Castle Rock has been occupied, perhaps even continuously, since at least the Bronze Age, around 3,000 years ago, and even before that its location must have made it attractive to humans. Throughout history, all over the planet, people have been attracted to accessible high places. While much has been made of the military advantage of such locations, and Edinburgh Castle does indeed have a pronounced military history, there are reasons other than defence for people to come to such places.

Apart from the view, which allows weather patterns and people, either on foot, on horseback or in boats, to be seen approaching from many miles away, hilltop sites have, since the earliest human times, often had some sort of sacred role. It seems to be a common psychological trait for people to choose high places as holy places and it is fitting that the highest point of the Castle Rock is now occupied by St Margaret's Chapel. The oldest building on Castle Rock, the chapel was preceded by another dedicated to an earlier Christian saint, St Monenna, and before that it is very likely that there was some sort of pagan sanctuary there. It was the stated policy of the early Christian church to take over pagan sites, and in taking over the towering summit of Dun Edin the church was making a clear statement. St Monenna herself seems likely to have been modelled on an earlier pagan figure and through her association with a group of nine women is linked to an idea that is at least 15,000 years old and occurs in societies all over the world.

When the weather is clear, the view from up on Castle Rock is fantastic. Notable hills and mountains such as North Berwick Law to the east, the Paps of Fife to the north, Ben Ledi, Ben Lomond and Ben Arthur to the west, and far to the north, Schiehallion, the Fairy Hill of the

Caledonians, can all be seen. Many of these repetitous hills and mountains have their own stories to tell. In the past, at the biannual feast days of Beltain, May 1st, and Samhain (So-ween), the modern Halloween, many of these hilltops would have been ablaze with the ancient neid-fire. This was the old pagan fire of blessing, raised by friction, which was used to guard against evil and call for prosperity in the coming season. Such fires were still being lit into the 19th century, and in Scotland the past is never far away. It is quite likely that such fires blazed once on Castle Rock as they do nowadays on Calton Hill in the revived annual Beltain ceremonies.

As the story of the Castle Rock unfolds we will draw upon ancient traditions, archaeology, history and even some tales that might be little more than gossip. However storytelling is never just entertainment, and for stories to survive over time they have to remain relevant to the people both telling and listening to them. In one way history is the tale of those who consider themselves important, the kings, queens, prelates and the rich who swarm around them. Stories, on the other hand, generally passed down verbally from one generation to the next, tell us of the lives of the majority of people, the common folk. Stories also tell us how people in bygone times saw their world and their place in it, and how that world itself had come about. Nowadays we read our stories in books, but for untold millennia the only way that knowledge of the past and how to live in the present could be handed on was through the telling of stories. With the coming of books, history began to dominate but even today, in the most modern of cities, stories live on because people tell them to their children and their friends as they always have, and as they always will.

the name

THE NAME EDINBURGH CAN be traced back to the days when the people living in the area spoke a P-Celtic language. Nowadays the best-known P-Celtic language is Welsh, although a related form of language, Q-Celtic, survives as modern Scots Gaelic and Irish. The language the tribal peoples in the Lothians spoke 1,500 years ago was very much like an old form of Welsh and was probably a local dialect of the language spoken by most of the people in Scotland at the time. The Picts, a term used by the Romans (probably mishearing a native name like Pecht) for all the tribes north of Hadrian's Wall, were predominantly P-Celtic speaking while the Scots in Argyll spoke an old form of Gaelic, the surviving Q-Celtic language. Sources surviving in Welsh give us names like 'Minas Eidyn', the hill of Etin and 'Dinas Eidyn', the fort or seat of Etin. From as early as 638 AD we have a Latin reference to '*obsessio etin*', a siege of Etin, probably referring to a siege of Castle Rock. The term 'Etin' survives in a story of a three-headed Scottish giant and in a scattering of place names across the south of Scotland, it is possible that it was originally some kind of tribal name.

It was much later that the form 'Edinburgh' came into being, which led to the misguided notion that the name might mean Edwin's Burgh. The idea that Scotland's capital city and her magnificent Rock might have been named after a Northumbrian king is simply daft! As we shall see, the other name from the early Middle Ages, 'Castrum Puellarum' or the Castle of Maidens, links the castle and the city to very old ideas indeed.

st monenna

IN THE 13TH AND 14TH centuries Edinburgh
Castle was referred to as 'The Castle of Maidens'
or in Latin, 'Castrum Puellarum'. An old piece of
local folklore told that this was because it was
where the Pictish kings used to keep their
princesses. The root of the name, however,
appears to lie in its association with St Monenna.
In fact the name is probably linked to what
seems to have been one of the most ancient and
mysterious cults ever to have existed, that of the
Nine Maidens. Like many, essentially mythical,
early Scottish saints, Monenna is said to have
come over from Ireland with a group of nine
women. She had dedicated her life to spreading
the Christian gospel and in time she had chapels
dedicated to her on Edinburgh Castle Rock,
Dumbarton Rock, Stirling Rock, and Dundonald
in Ayrshire, all sites of ancient forts or
settlements. Monenna was dedicated to serving
her Christian God and therefore would have no
association with men. However, she was a
beautiful young woman and had been sought
after by many young, and not so young, men in
her native Ireland. She had of course spurned

them all, having decided to devote her entire life to God.

On arriving in Galloway Monenna and her companions began to preach the world of the Lord, but it wasn't long before the beauty of this devout young woman was noticed and commented upon. Monenna had set up her chapel on the western shores of Luce Bay in the south-west of Scotland and when a local chieftain, a young and healthy man in his twenties, heard of this new arrival and came to check on the reports of her beauty, he fell in love with her at first sight. He asked one of her companions to tell her that he wanted to speak to her and as she came to meet him he fell on one knee, took her left hand in both of his and said, 'Fair Monenna, I have never beheld one so lovely as you, and I would like you to become my wife.' Monenna pulled her hands away and stepped back.

'I have no interest in being any man's wife,' she said, bowing her head, 'I have dedicated my life to serving Christ. Now please leave.' She turned on her heel and disappeared into the small chapel.

However the young man was not so easily refused and over the next few weeks he kept coming back to the chapel and attempting to speak to Monenna. Her companions tried to keep him away but he would not be put off. It was clear that he had set his heart on making Monenna his wife. Monenna herself prayed and prayed for guidance and after one particularly distressing visit it came to her what she must do. She called her nine companions to her and said: 'You must follow me and trust me completely. This man has made our stay here impossible and if we are all to fulfil our vows to God we must go and preach in some other place.' She led them down to the beach and onto a large rock that was half submerged in the water. 'Now,' she said, 'I want you all to pray with me,' and she bowed her head. As the group of women prayed with bent heads there on the rock, a wondrous thing happened. The rock began to float and within minutes it was drifting away from the land. Right across the 30 mile wide Luce Bay, the great rock floated with its precious cargo, eventually coming to shore at Farnes, now part of Glasserton parish, not far from the famous Isle of Whithorn where St Ninian had his church. Here they thought they would be safe from the attentions of the love-struck chieftain.

However, the chieftain was a man of strong will and used to having his own way. Hearing of how Monenna and her companions had floated away on the tide he decided to follow her, miracle or no miracle. A couple of days after the group of women had landed, they began to build a simple wattle and daub church, plastering clay onto woven wooden hurdles, at a spot not far from where they had come to shore. They were all busy at their work when one of them called out to Monenna.

'Mistress, look,' she shouted, pointing to the north. 'He has come again.'

There in the distance was the mounted figure of Monenna's suitor, accompanied by half a dozen warriors. The armed warriors rode up to the women and the chieftain dismounted. He came forward to Monenna and again getting down one knee he said, 'I respect your devotion, sweet Monenna, but is it not true that the Lord has made us man and woman that we may populate the earth? I love you with all my heart and I promise that I will be a good and faithful husband to you, for is it not written that we should go forth and multiply? Please, dear Monenna, re-consider and be my wife.'

It was clear that he had taken advice from a priest or monk, and had put a lot of thought into his speech. Monenna panicked, she thought she could never get away from this ardent would-be suitor and she turned and ran away from the shore. Her companions made to follow her but at a word from their chieftain the warriors ran between the maidens and the fleeing Monenna. The chieftain himself ran after her up a small rise towards a group of blackthorn trees. By now Monenna was shaking with fear, sure that in his obsession with her this young man would take her by force. Reaching the copse of trees, and ignoring the thorns tearing at her clothes and her flesh, Monenna clambered up the tallest of the blackthorn bushes and clung to a sturdy branch, dishevelled and bleeding.

The young man came up to the clump of bushes. 'Oh Monenna, do not be afraid of me, I wish you no harm. I want only to make you happy and to live our lives as man and wife.'

As she heard him speak the fear left Monenna and she felt herself grow very calm. She felt absolutely certain that whatever happened she would be safe, for the Lord would protect her. She looked down at the smiling man and asked him,

'What is it about me that you love so much that you must pursue me against my, and God's, will?'

His smile grew broader as he replied. 'My lovely Monenna, ever since I first looked into your eyes I have been able to think of nothing but you and my love for you. You have the most beautiful and tender eyes in the all the world, and they tell me you have a pure, sweet heart.'

'So it is my eyes that you love?' Monenna asked in a strangely calm and detached voice.

'Well, it's not just your eyes, but they are what caught my heart, my love...' His words dried up as he saw the young woman in the blackthorn bush reaching out to break off two long thorns. Whatever could she be doing?

'So it is my eyes that have laid the spell of love on you?' Monenna said, and without a moment's hesitation, and looking at her suitor all the time, she stabbed the thorns into her eyes, twisted them and tore her beautiful grey-green eyes from their sockets. With the blood pouring down her face she held the blood-dripping thorns with their grisly trophies towards him. 'Here, you can have my eyes. Now leave me alone.'

The poor man almost fainted, he fell to his knees and was violently sick. He realised now that there was no way he could ever make this woman his wife. She was clearly mad. Stumbling, he turned away and headed back to where the others were, leaving Monenna sitting in the blackthorn, her sightless orbs trickling blood. He went back to his companions, they all mounted their horses and rode off, never to bother Monenna again. Her horrified companions came running up to help her from the tree.

'Worry not, maidens,' she said as her foot touched the ground, 'It is God's will and all shall be well, you will see.' And she was right, for due to this remarkable testimony of her devotion to the cause of Christianity, Monenna herself was the subject of one of God's miracles. She asked to be taken to the nearby well where she bathed her sightless sockets and woke up the following day with her eyes and her sight restored. In support of this tale there is the fact that the well, and many others that were dedicated to Monenna, were traditionally used by people who had trouble with their sight.

The other sites dedicated to St Monenna, like Stirling and Dumbarton Rock and Traprain Law, near Haddington in East Lothian (which is visible from the castle) were all sites of great importance to the tribal peoples of first millennium Scotland. These dedications echo many other sites and stories that relate to groups of nine women, sometimes associated with single powerful females. One such group was Morgan and her eight sisters who were said to inhabit the sacred island of Avalon, where they took Arthur after his last battle with Mordred at Camlaan. It is an interesting fact that when the site of St Margaret's Chapel, the oldest building in the Castle, was excavated in 1854, all the skeletons found buried there were female. Another story claims that there was a nunnery here long, long ago but that the nuns had to be moved elsewhere because of the attentions of amorous soldiers from the Castle.

the warriors of the Gododdin

THE MILITARY HISTORY OF Edinburgh's Castle Rock can be traced back a long time. As a place of such significance, it seems fitting that it is mentioned in the oldest surviving poem in Scotland, if not in the whole of the British Isles. The poem is called 'Y Gododdin' and survives in Welsh. Written at the end of the 6th century when the language spoken throughout southern Scotland was what is now called 'Archaic North Brythonnic', an ancestor tongue of modern Welsh, the poem details a tragic raid by the warriors of the Gododdin. This name is probably the origin of the Roman term, 'Votadini', which they applied to the tribal peoples of south-eastern Scotland. Like their cousins the Britons of Strathclyde and the Pictish tribes to the north, the Gododdin were a Celtic-speaking warrior people, made up of a series of tribes, clans or kin-groups. Their languages, like modern Welsh, were called P-Celtic to differentiate them from the Gaelic tongues of the Scots, Irish, and Manxmen, which are known as Q-Celtic. In the period in which the poem was

composed, what we now call southern Scotland
was in a state of major upheaval. The Anglian
tribes of north-east England were beginning to
merge together into an early form of kingdom
and throughout the 7th century they attempted
to take control of all the neighbouring lands.
In this period most people were still living in
tribal societies and it is from these roots that the
heroic poetry so well preserved in the Gododdin
arose. Like a great deal of early Welsh poetry it is
concerned with the actions of the 'Gwr Y Gogledd',
the Men of the North, the tribal warriors of
Lothian and Strathclyde. To date most scholars
of the period have thought that the battle
described took place in England near Catterick.

The warriors of the Gododdin assembled at
the mountain court of Din Eidyn, their name for
Edinburgh's Castle Rock. Present were many
famed warriors, Caradawg and Madawg, Pwl
and Euan, Gwyn and Gwion, men well versed in
the arts of battle and known for their courage
and skill. Among them was the Bard Aneurin,
himself no mean warrior, and it is from his song
that the words of the great poem are remembered
down the centuries. It was a great meeting at Din
Eidyn, warriors had come from far and near to

mount a raid against the encroaching Angles from the south. Some had come from as far away as Wales and Cornwall to help their cousins. Some were Gaelic-speaking Scots from Dalriada in the west and there was a handful of wild Pictish warriors from the north. These were all men who had been raised in the way of the warrior, had taken part in many raids and had, in earlier times, even raided one another. Warriors proved their skill and courage in the raiding of other tribes' cattle and when called to fight each man would choose his enemy and be true to the honour code of the tribes they fought man to man. These were battle-hardened men and men whose sense of honour was strong. None would follow any other whom he did not respect, and the first loyalty was to one's own honour, then to one's immediate kin and then to the tribe.

There they gathered for a mighty raid, men of different bloods, as keen on feasting as on battle. And what a feast there was at Din Eidyn in that fateful time! The warriors had assembled as their ancestors had done when the Roman legions tried to conquer Scotland all those centuries before. Now they convened for a full year, and it was Northumbrians from the south who were threatening, not to raid, but to try to conquer and control the warriors of the North. They must be stopped. So the warriors gathered and feasted at the high mountain court of Din Eidyn, mead and ale flowed like water and the food was the finest. The feast had been long in preparation and as the warriors caroused they listened to the bards sing of the great deeds of their ancestral heroes, above all Arthur, the god-like warrior whose courage and skill were an example to all.

After long months feasting, the warriors, three hundred of them, clad in their bright mail coats and shining helmets, with golden torques around their necks, went in ranks to be blessed by the priests before heading off to battle. For they knew well that they could not all return. Some, they knew, would become food for the ravens on the battlefield, but none knew that bright day just how many would be left on the field. Like their pagan ancestors for generations untold, these men had no fear of death in battle, in fact it was a fitting climax to the life of a warrior. Many of them thought it better by far to die in the glory of war, in the full vigour of one's strength than to waste away as an old man, racked by aches and pains, unable to mount a horse or swing a blade, dreaming only of past glories. Death in battle was an honour and made one a fitting subject for the songs of bards to inspire the generations to come. And so they rode off, well armoured in their chain-mail hauberks and helmets, each man with his own favourite weapon, sword or spear, battle-axe or lance, and each man astride his favourite horse. South they went by passes through the hills, sometimes in sunshine, sometimes in rain, camping out in tents or under the stars, singing the songs of their fathers as they went. For as their ancestors before them, they were mighty warriors, off to find glory in battle.

And at last they came to the plain where the Angles waited for them, well warned by their scouts of the approaching war-band. They were ready for battle with their men arranged in rings of shields, earthen walls raised against the charge of the Gododdin men. They had numbers far beyond those of the Men of the North, but battle commenced and warrior fought warrior. Gwaradur and Owen were fierce in battle, cutting down the flower of the Saxon force. But for every man that fell another took his place. Great were the skills of Caradawg and Madawg, Pwll and Peredur and at the end of the first day's fighting as the truce fell, their swords had spilt much Saxon blood. But many friends were gone, mere food for the corbies on the battleground. And so the next day and the next. The Gododdin fought like heroes, but they were outnumbered, and each day's dawning saw fewer and fewer of the heroes from the north rise to take their place against the foe. Gwaradur fought like a lion, rallying his cousins around him and never stepping back. But great warrior and leader though he was, he was no Arthur, no hero from the mists of time to stop the slow defeat of the Gododdin. For a full seven days the battle was fought, until at the last the Gododdin were no more. Honoured they were by their enemies, the fallen strength of the tribes there, and hardly a man left of their hundreds.

One man did leave the battle, a man whose fame the Saxons knew, a man whose name rings down the centuries from that fateful day. He had fought alongside his cousins, his friends, and brothers, only to see them all fall. Not for him though the glory of a warrior's death amongst his kin, at fateful Catraeth, for he had more work yet to do. He was Aneurin, bard of the Gododdin, and to him fell the sad task of commemorating his fallen companions in song. It was a work of sorrow, to sing the praise of those mighty men. Singing as they struck their foes down, as brave as wild boars defending their young, they fought on valiantly to their end. So he returned alone to the great fortress of Din Eidyn to compose a song that would inspire generations of warriors to come, to place the dead men's names in the pantheon of heroes, and to give glory to the brave warriors who fell together at Catraeth. In no more than a generation the Gododdin were over-run from the south, and even the language of the poem in time died out. But wherever Welsh has been spoken, the glory of these men has been sung and in their homeland, once the Picts finally defeated the Angles many years later, the story of the great battle was remembered, and still is to this day.

a grim tale

BACK AT THE END of the 10th century, it is said
that the Castle was occupied by Grim, a warrior
who had usurped the crown. He, like many of his
contemporaries, was extremely fond of hunting
and in the periods when he was not busy with
affairs of state, such as repelling raids from
Scandinavia, he spent a great deal of time in the
forests south of Edinburgh. At that time the word
'forest' meant any large area of uncultivated
ground, though much of Scotland's countryside
was heavily wooded. One of Grim's associates
had the appropriate name of Hunter and had
been given control of the area of Polmood south
of Biggar, where the king often came to hunt deer,
wild boar and even the wild cattle which were
still found in Scotland. While the King pursued
this sport his poor queen was left alone in the
castle, and she grew to resent the time her
husband spent hunting. It became a cause of
disagreement between them but Grim, as king,
felt he could do just as he liked and refused to
listen to his wife's complaints.

On one of his sojourns in the forest of
Polmood, Grim, accompanied only by Hunter

and a couple of men-at-arms, passed a humble house near Badlieu on the slopes of Clyde Law. As they rode by, a young woman came out of the door of the house. She was tall, with deep auburn hair and green eyes, and in the first flower of her youth and beauty. Grim felt his heart rise and the young lass looked back at this armed man on his magnificent stallion, thinking he was rather agreeable looking even if he was quite old. Grim smiled and nodded to the delightful creature and she smiled back at him as he rode off. For the rest of the day Grim could not keep his mind on hunting, time and again his thoughts returned to the beautiful girl he had seen earlier. Who was she? With her glorious red hair loose about her shoulders she had clearly not yet donned the headdress of a married woman. Hunter noticed that Grim was distracted and when he was asked to find out all he could about the young lass, he immediately sent one of the men-at-arms to enquire at the house. It transpired that the young lady was called Bertha and she lived alone with her aged father there on the slopes of Clyde Law. As Grim had noticed, she was yet unmarried and once she realised who was showing an interest, she made it clear that the older man's attentions were not unwelcome.

From that time on the queen in Edinburgh Castle grew more and more angry as her husband's hunting trips became more frequent. Soon he was spending almost all of his time at the chase. In her frustration the queen began to suspect that Grim was chasing more than deer and resolved to find out the truth. It was easy enough to be sure that he was spending his time in Polmood forest and once she had established that, she sent a couple of spies south to find out what was happening. When her spies returned it was to confirm her worst suspicions. Her husband was openly living in the forest with a beautiful young woman. They reported that they had gone to the house at Badlieu, by now a much more comfortable place than when Grim had first ridden by, and they had seen that the young woman was with child. The queen's blood froze in her veins and a great hatred rose in her heart against this young woman whom she had never seen. As the weeks passed and her husband hardly even informed her of his whereabouts the queen's hatred and frustration increased, and she wanted revenge on the girl who had stolen her husband's heart.

Then one day word came to the Castle that

the Danes were back, a large force of them had landed in East Lothian and seemed intent on spreading throughout the country. This was not simply a plundering raid but a major strategic move that was intended to test the very strength of the kingdom. Grim was sent for at once and the following day he arrived, stern-faced and prepared for battle. It took only a few days to send out the messengers to rally as many fighting men as could be gathered and Grim headed east to confront the invaders. A great battle took place and after losing many of his best and bravest men Grim at last triumphed, slaughtering the Danes in their thousands and burning their long-ships on the beaches of East Lothian. Exhausted by his efforts, as he had been to the fore throughout the battle, Grim headed back towards Polmood. Nothing would please him more than to see his beautiful Bertha and their infant son while he recovered from the battle. But when he got to the house on Clyde Law, it was empty. Near the door was a freshly raised mound. Fearing the worst, Grim ordered his men to open up the mound. There to his horror were the bodies of Bertha, her son and her old father. Taking advantage of her husband's absence, the queen had hired a group of bandits to carry out her vengeful whim. In an effort to hide their crime the assassins had buried the bodies and fled south to England, leaving just one of their number to report back to the queen.

There before the opened grave of his sweetheart Grim fell to his knees and hammered the ground with his fists. His men watched in silence as their king gave full vent to his grief. Then he leapt on his horse and headed north. He had a very good idea who had been behind this vicious action. He rode furiously along the forest tracks, coming over the Lammermuir Hills and seeing the great Castle of Edinburgh in the twilight. Soon he was at the gates of the castle itself where he saw a great black banner flying over the castle's highest tower. What was going on? What treachery was afoot? Jumping from his horse he ran into the castle, sword in hand, to be met on the causeway just inside the gate by his steward.

'Why is that banner flying?' He demanded, 'and where is the queen?'

The steward bowed his head and tentatively said, 'I am sorry to tell you, Sire, but the queen is dead. That is why I raised the black banner.'

'When did she die?' said Grim slowly.

'Just yesterday, Sire,' came the reply. 'She had been in a strange mood ever since a messenger came three days ago. At first she seemed happy at his news but once he had gone, she changed. All the colour left her cheeks and within hours she took to her bed. There was nothing we could do.'

'What do you mean?' asked Grim.

'Well sir,' the man said and hesitated, 'the Queen had lost the will to live.'

Perhaps it was remorse at the evil act she had committed that made her lose all interest in life but she was not the only one. Only a few days later Grim summoned his warriors and headed west to find Malcolm III, the true heir to the throne. It was said he sought battle to still his mind and escape his grief. Whatever the reason, Grim had changed; never a charismatic man, he was now prone to black moods and bursts of viciousness. Even before he found Malcolm and went into battle many of his men began to resent him. As the battle approached they began to drift away and in the battle itself many more fled. At last, alone and wounded, Grim was taken prisoner by Malcolm's men. Malcolm's hatred of the man he considered a usurper meant there would be little mercy. Once he had been crowned as Malcolm III he turned to vengeance. A surly and silent Grim was brought before his conqueror in Edinburgh Castle where he had so lately ruled and there, before the assembled court, he was blinded with hot irons and thrown into the dungeon where he died in grief and misery a few days later.

death of a queen

ON A COLD WET DAY in June 1093 a group of people were gathered round a simple bed in a room in the castle. On the bed lay Margaret, wife of Malcolm III King of Scots, known as 'Canmore', or the Big Chief. Her husband had gone south to battle against the English with their two eldest sons Edward and Edmund. It was clear that the queen was very ill and that she didn't have long to live. Already her name was a by-word for Christian devotion and amongst the small gathering by the bed were a couple of priests, one of them her closest adviser and almost constant companion, Bishop Turgot. Here on the Castle Rock she had raised a chapel to the Virgin Mary, inspired by its ancient name the Castle of Maidens and its legendary association with Sir Galahad and the devout St Monenna centuries before. Margaret was born in far off Hungary, where she had spent her childhood, before coming to England with her brother Edgar Atheling, grandson of King Edmund II, who became the heir to King Edward the Confessor. Sadly he had never had a chance to rule due to the invasion of the Normans in 1066 under William the Bastard,

Duke of Normandy. Within a couple of years Margaret and her brother were driven from England and had sailed up the east coast and landed on the shores of the river Forth, with only a few companions. Today the spot where they landed is known as St Margaret's Hope and is close to the village of North Queensferry.

By then Margaret was a young woman, but she never had thoughts of marrying and having children. She spent a great deal of time in prayer and contemplation and it was her deep belief that she was destined in time to enter a nunnery, to spend the rest of her life in devotion to her Lord. That was before she met Malcolm Canmore. On hearing that Edgar had landed with no arms or money it might have been prudent for Malcolm to behave carefully. However, he had already made up his mind that he would support the rights of Edmund Ironside's grandson against the incoming Normans, if asked. So he was quite prepared to treat the tired, hungry and dispirited band of travellers with all the respect due to them as a royal company. He had Edgar and the others brought to his fortress on Castle Rock to greet them formally. As soon as he saw her, he fell in love with Margaret. She was grateful for the help and support provided for her family though taken aback at first by the king's obvious interest in her, but perhaps because of the good she knew it would do her brother, she decided to at least be pleasant to the king. A short time afterwards they were married and in time she became the mother of eight children, two of whom went on to become Kings of Scotland.

Margaret never lost her passion for religion and founded a great Abbey at Dunfermline, a few miles from the north coast of the River Forth where she first entered the country of Scotland. This soon became a place of pilgrimage, like St Andrews to the northeast. In order to help the many devout Christians who wanted to visit such places the Queen started and maintained a ferry across the Forth, close to her original landing spot, thus giving us the names of the modern towns of North and South Queensferry. Having lived a life of luxury and refinement Margaret was taken aback at just how rough and ready life at the Scottish court could be. She is said to have stopped the common practice of throwing meat bones to the dogs which sat around the dining tables and, even more significantly, she is credited with having started the practice of putting buttons on the sleeves of shirts and jackets. This was to stop the courtiers wiping their noses and mouths on their sleeves, a practice the genteel Margaret found rather offensive.

Margaret's whole life had been affected by battle and dynastic squabbling and now as she lay on her deathbed, she feared for the lives of her husband and sons fighting in England. Then her son Edmund arrived in the small chamber in the Castle.

'My son, I am glad to see you,' she said softly, as she lay clutching a large and ornate cross, 'How are your father and brother?'

'They are well,' replied a grim-faced Edmund, looking hard at his brothers and sisters around the bed.

'I am close to meeting the Maker myself,' she said, smiling gently, 'and I have felt what has happened. Tell me.' Reluctantly the exhausted Prince confirmed that both his father and brother Edward had been killed in battle. To add to their troubles he had learnt on arrival that his uncle Donald Bane, Malcolm's half-brother, was heading for Edinburgh with the intention of taking the crown. Under the old ways of tribal Scotland, as the king's brother, he was next in succession, being closer to their ancestors than any of his nephews. Donald had an army of tribal warriors from various parts of Scotland, whereas most of Malcolm's forces were either dead or scattered through the Borders after the disastrous battle at Alnwick. There was no way that Edmund could gather enough men to fight Donald and uphold his own claim to the throne.

Margaret took the news quietly, though as she closed her eyes momentarily a tear ran down her cheek. She opened her eyes. 'Whatever happens, it is the will of the Lord. Remember children to pray to the Lord, to be good and that I love you all, now and forever.' At that she closed her eyes and a great breath left her body. The queen, soon to be canonised as St Margaret, was dead. Now word came that Castle Rock was surrounded by Donald Bane's army. Bishop Turgot took command. He knew that the Queen's wish was to be taken to Dunfermline and buried in the abbey there. He would fulfil her wishes or die in the attempt. Quickly he summoned the queen's attendants and told them to prepare her body. All the necessary preparations were made and she was washed and dressed in the finest of robes. But just as the body was ready to be moved the sentries brought word that the weather was changing. The mist that had been swirling around all day had thickened and a vast blanket of fog was creeping up over the Castle rock. 'May God be blessed,' said the bishop, falling to his knees and crossing himself. Outside the besiegers doubled the guards at the front gates and on the north side of the Rock where there was a dangerous path from the castle. What they did not know was that there was small postern gate on the northeast corner of the battlements. On checking this, Edmund and his brothers found that it wasn't guarded. So, under the cover of thick fog the small party carried the body of the queen out from the Castle and off to the north. As they travelled it was as if the fog grew thicker behind them and a few hours later they reached the shore of the Forth. Here the Queen's Ferry carried the body of the queen over the waters to the little bay where she had first landed in Scotland, from where she was safely carried to Dunfermline. For centuries after that her tomb was the site of a great pilgrimage tradition, and on the top of Edinburgh Rock the chapel raised by St Margaret still stands today, the oldest surviving building in the castle.

william douglas takes the castle

THROUGHOUT THE 14TH century Scotland was almost constantly at war with her southern neighbour. English kings since the time of Edward I had regularly been trying to conquer Scotland, going so far as to invent historical reasons, with accompanying forgeries, for claiming feudal over-lordship of the country. As far back as the 7th century the Northumbrians had tried to conquer the Pictish tribes who lived in Scotland, and the struggle to resist being swamped by the larger and more powerful country to the south was a dominant part of Scottish political life right up to the Treaty of Union in 1707. However, back in the 1340s England, due to a series of invasions, still retained control of several important locations in Scotland. One of these was Edinburgh Castle, the most important castle in the entire country due to its command over the capital city. That the greatest castle in all of the country remained under English control was like a raw wound to many of the Scots, none more so than William, Earl of Douglas. Well known as a brave soldier and man of action, he decided to do something about it. A direct assault on the castle, if successful – and there was no guarantee of victory – would be costly in terms of men and materials. He had to come up with some way of getting into the castle whilst the entire garrison were not manning the walls. He discussed the matter with his close friend William Fraser of Cowie and Durris, and they came up with a plan. If they could convince the garrison that they were English merchants they might just be able to persuade them to grant them entry to the castle.

English ships were still regularly seen in the Forth at this time and there were always men looking to make a profit out of the ongoing war, so the plan was certainly not beyond the bounds of possibility. The pair rode north to Dundee where they hired a ship, which they decked out in English colours. They had plenty of experienced soldiers to call on, and the battle-hardened crew they drew together included John of Kinbuck, David Wate, William Bullock, and other very experienced soldiers. At this time most adult men in England had taken to shaving off their beards while in Scotland the old ways persisted and virtually every man was bearded, something that the English tended to look down as uncouth. In order for the plan to work it would be necessary for some of them to shave off their beards to pass as Englishmen. Luckily, Wate and Bullock had spent some time in England as hostages and were sure they could pass themselves off as northern Englishmen. Arriving in the Forth they dropped anchor off the island of Inchkenneth, and Wate and Bullock went ashore to make contact with the garrison in the castle. Now the countries were used to being at war but such was the intermittent nature of the ongoing struggle that at times things were quiet. Communications were slow and there were long periods of inactivity interspersed with bloody bouts of warfare. This was one of those periods of relative quiet and Wate had no problems in approaching the Castle. Although he believed that his years as a hostage in England should make convincing the garrison that he was an English merchant quite straight-forward, he was all too aware that he was putting his life on the line. He approached the castle and shouted to the guard he could see on the battlements above the main gate.

'Ho, friend, can I speak to the Commander of the garrison? I'm a merchant and my ship is out on the river stocked with provisions, and some fine drink too!'

'Wait there,' the guard shouted back and turned to speak to someone out of sight.

'Just wait a bit and the commander will be along presently,' the man called down.

A few minutes later Wate saw a well-dressed figure appear on a different part of the battlements and look out in the river, where the ship lay anchored, with an English flag flying at her masthead. The man looked and then turned and went out of sight. A few minutes later he appeared on the battlements above the gate.

'I am the Commander of the garrison in the King's name, who the devil are you?' he called down.

'My name is Tyler sir, I am a merchant and I thought you and your brave men would appreciate some good victuals.'

'How did you get here,' demanded the Commander.

'By Jove sir, it was a close thing but we can outrun any of these lubberly Scottish ships. I have the very best of food and drink on my ship in the river. I would like to make you a present of some of my merchandise to convince you of its quality.' Wate shouted back.

'That seems very fair of you,' called back the man above. 'Can you come back with the goods at about eight in the morning tomorrow?'

'That is no problem at all sir, I will return in the morning,' and waving happily at the man on the battlements, Wate turned and headed back to the ship. The first part of the plan had worked perfectly.

'Well?' said Douglas when Wate got back to the ship.

'Everything is just fine. John, myself and the other lads who have had a shave will take the goods up in the morning at eight o'clock.'

'Right then,' said Douglas with a smile. 'I'll take the rest of the lads up to the castle before dawn and we'll be just round the corner from the gate. If you can keep the garrison off for a couple of minutes we'll be with you and we can get right among them.' So under cover of darkness Douglas and over 50 heavily armed men made their way quietly up Castle hill and lay hidden from sight amongst the undergrowth just a couple of hundred yards from the Castle gate.

The sun came up and they lay there quietly as the sentries patrolled the battlements above them. Just before eight o'clock Douglas saw Wate's party

approach the Castle gate. There were a dozen of
them. All clean-shaven, dressed in the smocks
that merchants generally wore, and each of them
carrying a stout wooden staff. They were leading
a couple of heavily laden horses and looking
around then as they came, to give the impression
of keeping a look out for unfriendly natives.
They neared the gate. 'Halloo,' cried Wate to the
sentry. 'The Commander is expecting us. Open
the gate.' Douglas and the others heard the
rattling of chains as the great heavy portcullis
was lifted to allow the merchant party into the
castle. 'Ready lads,' he whispered to the men
near him, 'Pass the word. We're about to go in.'

As the great gate was lifted Wate and Bullock
came forward leading the packhorses, with the
other men close behind them. There on the
causeway were a couple of relaxed looking
English soldiers, peering at the goods on the horses,
particularly the second one which seemed to be
carrying a couple of very large jars. They didn't
know what hit them. As soon as the last man
was through the gate Bullock ran and jammed
his staff directly under the gate. Another of the
men did the same thing at the other side of the
gate. As his companions ensured the gate could

not be dropped Wate whirled his staff up in the air and brought it crashing down on the head of the sentry nearest him. The man fell like a sack of potatoes and his companion had no time to cry out before he was felled by one of the others. Quickly they pulled out the swords hidden on the packhorse, as one of the men on the battlements above the gate let out a cry. This brought soldiers running down from the main body of the castle, about 30 of them. However, his cry had also alerted Douglas and the others, so the English soldiers racing down to repel what they thought was a small force of a dozen men soon realised that they had a real fight on their hands.

As the first of them ran to close with Wate and his men, Bullock ripped the jars from the second packhorse and threw them at the feet of the advancing soldiers. Half a dozen of them fell, tripping up their comrades behind them. This gave enough time for Douglas to reach the advance party and the combined force of Scots began to fight their way up the causeway into the main body of the castle. Seeing how the skirmish was going some of the English sentries took to their heels through the gate and down into Edinburgh. Such was the advantage of the surprise attack that some of the garrison were still asleep when they were taken prisoner. It a was a bloody but brief battle and soon the whole city of Edinburgh was out in the streets, cheering as the English flag was pulled down from above the ancient castle and the Scottish colours raised in its place.

the Black Dinner

EVER SINCE WILLIAM WALLACE had rallied the Scots against Edward Longshanks, King of England, in the closing years of the 14th century the Douglas family had held a noted place in Scotland. Sir William Douglas had fought alongside Wallace in his guerrilla campaign and on the battlefield, and his reputation as a brave and resourceful warrior passed on to succeeding generations. His family grew extremely powerful, and was often seen as a danger, and not just by the monarchs. They were equally feared by those amongst the leading families who sought to further their own power. Intrigue and plotting were a way of life amongst the so-called aristocracy of Scotland in the Middle Ages. Much was spoken of honour, but there were many black-hearted and backstabbing deeds that such words shielded. Perhaps no episode in the period shows the bloodthirstiness of the time so much as the fate of the sixteen-year-old William, Earl of Douglas in 1440.

William had succeeded to his title on the death of his father Archibald who had died in June that year. Archibald had been appointed lieutenant-governor of the kingdom on the

Coronation of James II, at the age of seven in 1439. Archibald was feared and hated by the official Regent, Sir Alexander Livingstone of Callender, and the Chancellor, William, Baron of Crichton, and this hatred extended to his son. Both of them were extremely ambitious but were united in their hatred and fear of Archibald and his power. With their extensive land and the hundreds of armed men always available to them from the Borderlands of Annandale and Galloway, the Earls of Douglas were powerful indeed. And they knew it. Archibald had shown his contempt for both the Regent and the Chancellor when he said, 'They are both alike to me, it is no matter which may overcome, and if both perish the country will be the better; and it is a pleasant sight for honest men to see such fencers yoked together.'

When Archibald died in June 1440 of natural causes, the biggest obstacle to the soaring ambitions of Crichton and Livingstone was removed. But they still had to deal with William, who although only 16 at the time, had been raised to take over the great power of the Douglas family. He could call upon the loyalty of many and was the natural focus for those who were opposed to the machinations of Crichton and Livingstone. They were further alarmed when William became caught up in the splendour and the trappings of power and wealth that were suddenly his to command. He took to appearing in public with a large company of heavily armed, well-mounted and magnificently-equipped men. He also took the opportunity to send Sir John Fleming and Sir John Lauder of the Bass to the court of the French king to ask for a new charter for lands that had been given to his grandfather by Charles v. This was clearly a young man who had every intention of exercising all the power and authority he could command. The Chancellor and the regent had hoped that with the death of Archibald they would have no trouble with the Douglas family for a while and were in a quandary. Any open attack on William would most likely plunge the whole country into civil war. They did not want to take on the power of the Douglases directly, the country had only just settled down after the troubles that had arisen from the assassination of James I. But something had to be done to rein in this ambitious and headstrong young man. Some have said that this plot against William included James Douglas, the Earl of Avondale and William's great-uncle.

Now, after the assassination of his father and the consequent turmoil in the country it had been felt that the best, and safest, place for the boy-king to be brought up was Edinburgh Castle. It was the biggest and best defended castle in the country, and the wily Crichton had effectively separated James from his mother and her courtiers who lived a mile away at Holyrood Palace. He was forever citing the need for absolute safety, and after Archibald's death he and Livingstone had the king completely under their own control. From their base in the country's greatest stronghold, the Chancellor and Regent hatched a plan to solve the problem with the Douglases. They knew how dangerous their actions would be, but in those bloody times, decisiveness was always seen as a virtue. An invitation was sent to William at his home at Restalrig, just a couple of miles from the Castle. Couched in the most glowing terms, it invited the Earl of Douglas, and his younger brother David, to a dinner with his sovereign James II at the Castle on 24 November 1440. Perhaps it was the confidence of youth, or maybe William truly thought that Crichton and Livingstone were interested in his opinion on the future of the country, we will never know, but

William accepted the invitation. He turned up at the castle with his usual company of attendant soldiers but entered the castle with only his brother and one other companion, Malcolm Fleming of Cumbernauld, a trusted adviser of his father's. He at least should have known better than to enter the lion's den so boldly! It is possible he did but that William's headstrong temperament over-ruled the sagacity of the older man. As it was there were only three of them who entered the castle that night.

Once they were in the castle the portcullis was gently lowered and the great gates quietly shut as they made their way up to the king's apartments. Here they greeted their sovereign, still only ten years old, and were seated at a great table groaning with silver and gold plate and dishes. A truly sumptuous banquet of several courses was served up. Then towards the end of the meal the atmosphere changed. As they sat there chatting with their young king William looked up to see two servants bringing in a large silver platter. On it was a black bull's head – an ancient symbol meaning only one thing. Death! The three men leapt to their feet, drawing their swords. Immediately the room was filled with fully armed and armoured men. As the young king shouted for it all to stop Fleming and the Douglas boys were overpowered and dragged out of the chamber. There in the Castle, where the barracks now stand, they were beheaded under the stars, Crichton and Livingstone looking on and ignoring the entreaties of James II. There was not even the pretence of a show trial. The Chancellor and the regent had decided that Douglas must die. A poem from the time tells of the widespread revulsion that arose in Scotland when news of the Black Dinner spread through the country.

> Edinburgh Castell, toun and tour,
> God grant ye sinke for sinne;
> And that even for the black dinour,
> Earl Douglas gat therein.

If Crichton and Livingstone thought this would consolidate their power and lead to peace they could not have been more wrong. Incensed by this treachery, the Douglas family and their friends rose in arms against them. Under the leadership of James Douglas the Earl of Avondale, who had succeeded to the leadership of all the Douglases as the seventh Earl of Douglas and Angus, the struggle for control of the young king continued and the country was in an almost constant state of turmoil for years. James II himself grew to fear and hate the Douglases and was instrumental in the death of James's son William, the eighth Earl of Douglas and Angus at Stirling Castle in 1552. However the Black Dinner is probably the most notorious episode in the entire history of Edinburgh Castle.

a ϑangeʀous man

KINGS OF SCOTLAND were often paranoid and none more so than James III. And he had good cause to be. In the months after his marriage to Margaret of Oldenburg, Princess of Denmark, in 1476, he became concerned that both his brothers, Alexander, Duke of Albany and John, Earl of Mar, were plotting against him. He grew to believe that Alexander was even plotting with the English to overthrow him and have himself crowned as King Alexander IV. This was all too believable as Alexander, who held the position of the Warden of the Marches and was thus responsible for maintaining peace along the border with England, was a wild and dangerous man. On many occasions he mounted major raids into England, not for any sound political reason but apparently to gather booty. In this he was assisted by a large group of men, little better than bandits, whom he had recruited amongst the wild families of the Borders. These families, like their distant cousins in the Highlands, were addicted to the raiding way of life, ever ready to take advantage of the chaotic situation arising from the regular outbreaks of hostilities between Scotland and England, and were a constant problem to both north and south.

Albany, rather than controlling these bandits, seemed almost to have become one of them and carried out raids in Scotland too. James was becoming increasingly angry at this and in 1482 ordered the arrest of both of his brothers. John was said to have died of a fever soon afterwards and it was rumoured that the fever had been caused by witchcraft, while another even grislier tale claimed that he had been bled to death in the dungeons of Craigmillar Castle. Whatever his eventual fate, he disappeared for good shortly after being arrested. There are those who suggest that it was perhaps John's skeleton that was found walled up in the castle in 1818. Albany was committed to Edinburgh Castle where James reckoned he would be safe from any escape attempts by either his band of desperadoes or the more reckless of his supporters amongst the courtiers. While he had a faction of supporters Albany also had plenty of enemies at court, some of whom urged the king to try him for treason and execute him. Albany, being informed of the disappearance of his younger brother, was only too aware that the king was unlikely to be more

merciful towards him, particularly after his
behaviour as Warden of the Marches. He might
have been imprisoned but he was of the royal
blood and had a constant stream of visitors to
his rooms in the castle. These quarters were in a
long-since gone building known as David's
Tower which stood right on the edge of the
northern cliff of Castle Rock. Despite his royal
position, he was a prisoner and only had one
servant or chamber-chiel.

One evening he was told by a visitor that
there was a French ship that had brought a
consignment of wine from Gascony, anchored off
Leith. If he could make his way there the captain
was ready to take him out of Scotland, the
necessary bribes already having been paid. The
following day, two barrels of wine from the
Gascon ship arrived at David's Tower, and were
brought unopened to Alexander's apartments.
Hidden in one of them was a thin but strong
rope and a letter. The letter contained an ominous
message. It said that a group of the courtiers
around the king were urging that he should not
be tried, but killed out of hand and that the king
was minded to accept their advice. There was no
time to lose. He would have to try to escape. So

that night he invited the Captain of the Guard
and his three principal officers to sample the
wine that had been delivered. They were happy
to accept the invitation and that evening they
arrived, all wearing breastplates and helmets.
They took off their helmets and set to sampling
the Gascon wine and playing cards. Alexander
was careful to ensure that they all drank more
than he did and after a couple of hours all four
of the officers were considerably drunk. Three of
them were virtually comatose, and the Captain of
the Guard was the only one to still have his wits
about him to any extent. Judging his moment
Alexander grabbed the captain's long dagger from
his belt and stabbed him in the heart. Again and
again he stabbed him before turning his attention
to the others. Within a minute or two all had
suffered the same bloody fate. Whether fired up by
blood-lust or acting out of spite, it is impossible
to say, he and his servant threw the four bodies
onto the great roaring fire that blazed at one end
of the room. Then they headed to the top of the
windowless tower carrying the rope. Tying it to
the balustrade Alexander threw it over the side
and his servant went first over the battlements.
However, when he came to the end of the rope

he found himself still a distance from the ground. There was nothing to do but let go and hope for the best. He fell more than 20 feet and letting out a yell as his leg broke, rolled over, hit his head and lost consciousness. Above him Albany realised what must have happened. Not knowing whether anyone else had heard the cry he hurriedly pulled up the rope. Luckily he had thought to bar the door into the tower so he had some time if guards were coming. He ran back down to his chambers and using the captain's blood-encrusted dagger quickly cut his sheets and blanket into strips. By now sweating profusely, he hardly noticed the stench of the burning bodies that was beginning to fill the tower. Again he returned to the top of the tower and tied the sheets and blankets to the end of the rope, before once more flinging it over the battlements. The rope was now just long enough and soon he was standing at the foot of Castle Rock. In the darkness he could see that his servant was not only unconscious but that his leg was lying at an odd angle. Then showing a concern and humanity which was the opposite of his behaviour just a short time earlier, he hoisted the man on his shoulders and set off to Leith. Whatever else could be said of Albany, he was a strong and fearless man and when he put his mind to something he did it. Once in Leith he soon found a boat to take him and his injured servant out to the Gascon boat. By dawn he was safely out in the North Sea.

When the king heard of his brother's escape and the horrendous carnage he had left behind, he did not believe it until he had visited David's Tower for himself. There he saw the unfortunate guards' bodies 'roasting like tortoises in their shells', as an earlier historian described it. Albany went to France, but finding himself unable to convince the French king, Louis XI, to help him against his brother, departed for England where he was sure he would get help to depose James. Sure enough, Edward IV entered into a treaty with Alexander at Fotheringay in June 1482. He showed his true colours in agreeing to become the King of Scotland under the suzerainty or control of Edward, just like the earlier John Balliol who had similarly done homage to Edward I nearly a century earlier, which he too could never fulfil. Alexander's faction amongst the nobles in Scotland, hearing that he was coming north with a large army led by the Duke of Gloucester, later King Richard III of England, seized James and let it be known they would recognise Alexander as king, but not if he came into Scotland with Gloucester. There was great deal of communication between the various parties and in the end a truce was declared between the two countries, James was re-installed as king, Alexander was pardoned, all his lands and property restored and he was created the Earl of Mar and Garioch. Alexander, however, could not help himself and was soon dealing with the English behind James's back again. While in England, he was denounced as a traitor and condemned to death in Scotland. Again he came north on a raid into Scotland but was defeated by a force loyal to James at Lochmaben and fled to France where he met his death in a fitting manner – being accidentally killed at a jousting tournament. His elder brother only survived him by three years before falling to an assassin's knife during a battle with his still rebellious nobles. Such were the ways of kings and their kin in Scotland's Middle Ages.

lady Glammis

SCOTLAND'S HISTORY IS littered with bloody episodes. Centuries of invasions by the English were accompanied by civil strife between people of different religious beliefs, dynastic squabbles amongst the nobility and the ever-present inter-tribal raiding of the Highland and Border clans. However one of the most horrific and extended episodes was the persecution of the witches. The Christian Bible said 'thou shalt not suffer a witch to live', and in the period from around 1560 to the 1720s untold numbers of innocent women were ritually burnt for the supposed crime of witchcraft. Most of them were guilty of no more than using traditional spells and medicines, and some were likely to have been practising ancient pagan rites, but all were the focus of masculine hysteria against their supposedly Satanic practices. Many of them were undoubtedly informed against out of jealousy or hopes for personal gain. Although their accusers claimed that these unfortunate women consorted with Satan himself, the truth was often much more mundane. Many of the women were old and lived alone, and with no man to defend them were easy prey for all

sorts of ne'er-do-wells. Witchcraft could also be a
convenient cover for settling scores, the most
blatant case of this type resulting in the dreadful
spectacle of a beautiful young woman being
burnt in public at the gates of Edinburgh Castle
on 17 July 1537.

James v, like many medieval monarchs, was
constantly on the look out for treason. This
paranoia was justified, for throughout Europe
monarchies were anything but stable. Kings were
always wary of their more powerful nobles,
seeing in them potential challengers for their own
position. In many cases these nobles were related
to the kings by blood and had some sort of claim
to the throne themselves. In James' time the most
powerful family in the land were still the
Douglases, who a century before had been the
major threat to James's grandfather. In 1536 the
Master of Forbes and fifteen others had been
brutally executed for treason on trumped up
charges. They were hung, drawn and quartered,
a dreadful fate in which the victim was cut down
from the gibbet while still just alive then had his
stomach slit and his intestines pulled out and
burned before him. This was followed by
decapitation and dismemberment and in most

cases the display of the body parts on prominent
sites, such as city gates or castle walls. This
bloody act did not quieten the king's fears and
soon he turned his attention to the Douglases
again. This time his main target was Lady Jane
Douglas, the young and beautiful widow of John,
Lord Glammis. Being still in the flower of her
womanhood, Jane had re-married, her second
husband being Archibald Campbell of Skipness.
He had been considered very lucky for Jane was
a notable beauty whose looks and figure were
accompanied by a calm temperament, considerable
courage and a fine intelligence. And it seems her
beauty led to her downfall.

When Glammis died there were many men
who had tried to woo Jane and one of them was
William Lyon, whose jealousy of Campbell led
him to seek revenge. Lyon was well aware of the
King's constant fear of treason and he decided to
get his revenge not on Campbell but on Jane by
accusing her of treason, along with her young
son Lord Glammis and her old priest John Lyon.
Jane, Campbell, the young Lord Glammis and
the old priest were all arrested and locked up in
the Castle. Now James, like his predecessors, was
ever ready to believe ill of the Douglases at any

time, and by charging Jane he knew he would
also be damaging her brother, the Earl of Angus
and head of the Douglas family. Given that many
of his court and the people in the country at large
held Jane in high regard, he realised that it might
be hard to make such charges stick against her. It
was unlikely that people would believe she had
been plotting treason against the king. Her
character was impeccable, without blemish, and
she was very much respected by everyone who
knew her. So in order to ensure his case against
her was successful he added the charge of witchcraft. To get the testimony he needed to convict
her, the King resorted to torture. Her clansmen
and servants were put on the rack and stretched
to the point of agony, until they finally gave false
evidence against her. Then she too was subjected
to torture. John, her son, who was 16 at the time,
was forced to watch in horror, before being
brutally tortured himself. Using these savage
tactics the King got his confessions. Such was the
hysteria of the time that even the laying of such a
charge turned many of Jane's friends against her,
they wanted nothing to do with anyone who
dabbled with the Devil. And torture was the
norm to get confessions from so-called witches.

The justification given was that they were in the power of the Devil and the only way to overcome this power, and the Black Arts such creatures had been given by the unholy master, was to torture them. So from the evidence of her own lips she was convicted of witchcraft, and she was condemned to death.

She was a woman in the prime of her life and it seems that when she was brought out to be burnt alive on that fateful day she carried herself with courage and dignity, and despite the horror of witchcraft felt by almost the entire population there were many there that day who felt some degree of sympathy for this lovely woman. A large stake had been driven into the ground and surrounded by tar-coated bundles of sticks and barrels of tar. The executioners hoisted Jane up on top of the piled up barrels and wood and tied her firmly to the stake. Then they came down and in the sight of thousands of people who had gathered to watch they set fire to the pile. At once the wood burst into flame and great gouts of black smoke arose. Forced to watch from the window of a cell in David's Tower, her husband and son could do nothing to help her. The following night, Campbell, driven close to madness by grief, attempted to escape by climbing down the sheer face of David's Tower. There were those who said he wasn't really trying to escape, but to make it look like he had accidentally fallen to his death, suicide being such a dishonourable act. James, on hearing of this, decided that enough was enough and allowed Lord Glammis to live, the old priest being simply banished. Tellingly, the man who was supposed to have prepared the poison that Jane had been accused of ordering to assassinate the king, was also spared though he did suffer the indignity of having his ears cut off to mark him as a criminal. Lord Glammis was eventually released from the Castle after the death of James v in 1542. As for Lady Jane, it is said that she is the Grey Lady who, ever since, has sporadically haunted Glamis Castle 60 miles north of Edinburgh. Persecuted and judicially murdered while innocent of all charges brought against her, it would be little wonder if her spirit were indeed restless.

MONS MEG

THE GREAT CANNON that sits close to St Margaret's
Chapel, looking over the Firth of Forth from the
battlements of the castle, is known as Mons Meg.
Children from all over the world are disappointed
to learn that this is not the gun that fires a round
at one o'clock every day but Sunday. This is just
as well, for Meg is a very old piece of ordnance
and any attempt to fire her would undoubtedly
result in her blowing up. The story goes that this
massive piece of ordnance was made for James II
for a siege of Threave Castle in 1455 by Brawny
Kim McLellan, the smith of Mollance, near Castle
Douglas in the south-west of Scotland. The name
of the cannon was supposedly given because its
thunderous roar reminded the smith of the voice
of his good wife Meg. This siege of Threave
Castle was part of the ongoing struggles with the
Douglas family that saw so much bloodletting
and perfidy. James was particularly incensed that
the 8th Earl of Douglas had asked for help from
the English king, Henry VI, in the building of the
castle. This was one of the reasons the king was
directly involved in the Earl's assassination in

Stirling Castle in 1452. But, as ever, there was another Douglas ready to step up, and the 9th Earl was defiant in his resistance towards the king and had taken refuge in the castle. The huge cannon was dragged into position, a peck of powder, equivalent to two gallons dry measure, and a massive granite ball, said to have been as heavy as a Carsphairn cow, was loaded. The gunner blew on his match to get it burning bright and applied it to the great gun. Off went Meg with a roar, which seemed to shake the very earth itself. Margaret, the Fair Maid of Galloway, widow of the 9th Earl of Douglas was sitting sipping wine in the castle when the great ball is said to have ripped through the wall of the chamber and taken off her hand. Some say that as result of this the Douglases surrendered, but in truth it took two months and a great deal of bribery on the part of the king before the castle was surrendered. There are those that will tell you that one of the rings on the hand that was blown away was not only found, but is still in existence.

Whatever the truth of that, the king was definitely fond of Mons Meg and she was dragged all over the country, and into England, as he

continued the struggles to hold onto his throne.
As often as not on approaching a town, the great
gun would be bedecked in a scarlet and gold cloth
and preceded by pipers playing warlike tunes.
This popularity continued with James II's successors
and Meg became an icon in her own right. Her
sheer bulk of around six tons made her a suitable
symbol of royal authority. There are few records
of her usage other than at the siege of Norham
Castle on the Tweed in 1497, on another sally
against the English. No one knows how often she
was fired in anger, but 50 years later, Mons Meg,
whose great weight made it impractical to move
her any distance – the shot alone weighed up to
150 kilos – was brought back to Edinburgh Castle.
Surviving royal accounts from many of the later
reigns continue to show expenditure on her upkeep.
She was fired to celebrate the marriage of Mary,
Queen of Scots, to the Dauphin, the heir to the
French throne, on 24 April 1558. Twenty-three
years later the cannon was reloaded in the castle,
this time the salute was for James VI of Scotland,
and eventually in 1603, of England too. However,
the years had taken their toll on the old girl and
this time as she roared again, she blew apart.
Her barrel split and there was no chance she

could ever be used seriously again. Such was the affection that the King, and to some extent the people, held for Meg, that it was ordered that she be repaired.

In 1753 in the paranoia enveloping Scotland in the aftermath of the Jacobite Rebellion of Bonnie Prince Charlie, another Stewart who aspired to be a king, Meg was transported south to London. Perhaps she was seen as too strong a symbol of Scottish national consciousness, for there was no military value in a piece of ancient ordnance like auld Meg. Later, under the influence of Sir Walter Scott, who did so much to romanticise the true history of Scotland, Meg came back once more. Thus in 1829 horses once again dragged her into the castle preceded by pipers playing in her honour. As they had done so often in centuries past, the people of Edinburgh turned out to cheer the old lass as she was returned to the place of honour atop the battlements in the Castle. The inscription on the great gun rather contradicts some of this fine old tale, for it refers to the place of origin as Mons in Belgium. In truth she was one of a pair of bombards presented to James VI by his uncle, Phillip, the Duke of Burgundy, in 1457. However the story of Meg's origin passed into the folklore of Scotland and she did indeed become a national icon.

A PRINCE IS BORN

ON 19 JUNE 1566 Lord Darnley arrived in Edinburgh Castle, not long after nine in the morning. He had been summoned there to acknowledge the son that Mary Queen of Scots had just given birth to as his own. The birth of James VI of Scotland, who was later to become James I of the United Kingdom of England and Scotland, had been prophesied over three hundred years earlier by Thomas the Rhymer.

'My lord,' said the Queen, lying in her bed, 'God has given you and me a son, begotten by none but you.' Darnley blushed and leant forward to kiss the child in his cradle. The queen then had one of her maids hand the child to her and uncovering his face she went on, 'My Lord, here I protest to God and as I shall answer to him at the great day of judgement, that this is your son and no other man's son. And I am desirous that all my ladies and the others here bear witness, for he is so much your own son that I fear it will be the worse for him hereafter.'

She then spoke directly to Sir William Stanley, an English attendant of Darnley's, 'This is the son whom I hope shall first unite the two kingdoms of Britain.'

'Why, Madam,' replied Sir William, 'Shall he succeed before Your Majesty and his father?'

'Because,' said the queen sadly, 'his father has broken with me.'

This sad exchange at his birth reflects the turbulent times into which the future King of Scotland and England was born. Scotland itself was in chaos. In March Darnley had plotted with some of his friends, including the Earls of Lindsay and Gordon, who had led a group of armed men into the Queen's Chamber in Holyrood House and killed her secretary David Rizzio in front of her. The unstable and dangerous Darnley had already fallen out with the Queen and had decided that she was having an affair with her Italian secretary, despite her advanced pregnancy. The brutal slaughter of the Italian meant that any rapprochement between Mary and her King-Consort, Darnley, was now impossible.

The remarks made by the Queen and Darnley at his acknowledgement of James as his son were of great importance. Elizabeth, Queen of England, was single and showed no sign of ever marrying and producing an heir to the English throne. The next in line to the throne of England was in fact

Mary, through Henry VII of England, her great-grandfather. After her the next in line to the English throne was now the new baby, James. This was the future king of the Scots and, as his mother had hoped, he did go on to become the first King of both Scotland and England, putting an end to over a thousand years of bloody warfare as the Scots resisted all attempts to conquer them. It took a further hundred years and a great deal of bribery and coercion for the two countries to finally unite under the Act of Union of 1707, the true written constitution of the United Kingdom. That, however, was far in the future and Darnley's acknowledgement of his son made him, in essence, dispensable. Now he had provided and acknowledged an heir to the throne, he was of no further use to the Queen and her supporters.

The Queen had already, at the age of 24, had an extremely eventful life. She had become Queen of Scots at the age of six days old, her father James V dying in December 1542 not long after a heavy defeat by the English at the Battle of Solway Moss. She was crowned in a full ceremony at only nine months old and by then she had already been promised in marriage to Edward, son of Henry VIII of England. This union was intended to bring to an end a thousand years of struggle between the two countries by uniting them under one monarch. Henry VIII had famously split away from the Catholic Church and this union was fiercely opposed by Mary's mother, Mary of Guise, a devout French Catholic. As word got out of the intended eventual union of the monarchies there was a great deal of unrest. The country was already troubled by the struggles between the Catholic Church and the new Protestant reformers, but the people of Scotland were not ready to be brought under English rule, which was how the treaty was perceived. In fear of a general uprising the Scottish Parliament revoked the agreement for the marriage, which had the usual result. A series of raids by English armies took place to try and bend Scotland to Henry's will. This went as far as an actual attempt at kidnapping Queen Mary in 1554. However, in 1548 the French had a new king, Henri II, and he too saw potential in a marriage with the young Queen of Scots.

Scotland and France had long been allies, driven together by their common role as enemies of England, and Henri suggested a marriage with his son, the Dauphin or Crown Prince, Francois. This idea was of course very attractive to Mary of Guise and a treaty was signed agreeing to the marriage in 1548 at the nunnery near Haddington in East Lothian. Poor wee Mary was simply a political pawn at this stage. With the country under permanent threat of invasion from England, Mary of Guise sent her daughter to France where she stayed for ten years. Here she grew into a tall, beautiful, and highly accomplished young woman, who was very popular among the French courtiers. Apart from her skills as a musician, her horsemanship and needlework – nowadays a rather odd combination but quite normal then, at least for someone of her station – Mary was a fluent linguist, mastering English, French, Greek, Italian, Latin and Spanish in addition to her native Scots. In April 1558 at the age of 15 she married François and her future seemed assured. The following year her husband succeeded to the French Crown as Francois II and Mary was now Queen of Scots and of France. Sadly Francois died a couple of years later and his successor was still a child. Under the influence of Mary's mother-in-law, Catherine de Medici, the French agreed to withdraw the soldiers they had in

Scotland and to recognise Elizabeth 1 as Queen of England.

So when Mary returned to Scotland in 1561 she was already a widow, an ex-Queen and only 19 years old. Despite her accomplishments, the situation in Scotland was beyond her control. The struggles between the Catholics and Protestants were causing continuous strife and the troubles with England were never far away. Relations between Mary and her cousin Elizabeth in England never got beyond the level of mutual suspicion, and good advice was hard to come by for the young Queen. What seemed clear was that a suitable marriage might help stabilise the situation, at least in Scotland, and the birth of an heir was something everyone wanted. The lack of an heir in England was a disaster that was to be avoided at all costs. In 1565 Mary married a cousin, Henry Stuart, Lord Darnley, who was in fact an English subject. This infuriated Elizabeth who felt she should have been consulted about the marriage. She was also concerned that any child of the marriage would become the next heir to the English throne. As it was the marriage was a disaster. Darnley was an arrogant fop and was greatly resented by the Protestant faction at the

Scottish court. This led to Mary's illegitimate half-brother, the Earl of Moray, actually leading an open revolt, which was unsuccessful. However, the Protestant reformers were gaining in strength and popularity and their fiercest propagandist, John Knox, regularly preached against the Catholic queen.

This was the background to that fateful day when the future King James vi and i was born.

By August that year the Queen was discussing ways of escaping from her 'intolerable marriage' with her close advisers Sir William Maitland of Lethington and the Earls of Bothwell and Moray. Divorce, however, was impossible, as it would cast doubt on James' legitimacy and Mary was determined he would become the King of Britain in time. Matters were complicated by the obvious attraction between Bothwell and the Queen but it was clear that something would have to be done about Darnley, who was often seen drunk and boasting in the streets of Edinburgh. In a surprising act of clemency Mary pardoned Rizzio's murderers who had fled abroad. However, this was a cover for a more devious plan and on 10 February 1567 Darnley's house at Kirk o' Field was blown up, his body being found in the garden, showing signs of strangulation. In May Mary went on to marry Bothwell but this too was hardly a love match. It was also highly unpopular at both court and in the country at large, Bothwell being a Catholic. Over the next few years Scotland fell into a form of Civil War and the unfortunate queen was eventually forced to abdicate in favour of her infant son. Such was her unpopularity by this time that Mary was forced to flee to England, where any expectations of a hearty welcome were soon dashed. Elizabeth had her imprisoned as a threat to the safety of the kingdom, after all, Mary was a viable claimant to the English throne and as a Catholic was seen by the Protestant English as a disruptive influence and a positive danger to the state. The two queens never met and Mary, who at one point had looked as if she could have ended up as the Queen of a unified Scotland, England and France, remained imprisoned for the next 19 years. However, as long as she was alive she was a threat to Elizabeth and in 1587 she was charged with plotting to overthrow her cousin. Once she was charged it was obvious she would be found guilty, she wasn't even allowed to present a proper defence. The sentence too was a foregone conclusion and on 8 February Mary

Stewart was executed at Fotheringhay Castle, Northamptonshire. She said at her trial to the assembled nobles trying her, 'Remember, gentleman, the theatre of history is wider than the realm of England.' To the last she behaved with a remarkable grace and calmness but the execution itself was dreadful affair, the executioner having to take three attempts to behead her. As her head rolled to the floor her little dog, which had been hiding beneath her skirts rushed out, drenched in blood and, it is said, died of shock shortly after. One of the reasons she had to die was that she was a natural focus for the many Catholics who still lived in England and Scotland. In order that no relics of her could be circulated and used to spread dissent, every one of her possessions was burnt. During this her son was conspicous by his absence.

He had sent ambassadors to Elizabeth to ask that his mother's life be spared, but in truth their role was to ensure James's succession to the throne of England after Elizabeth died. After all, he was the next direct heir and had been brought up in a country that since 1559 had been Protestant, a matter of extreme importance to the English as a whole. It was his actions at his mother's death that have led to doubts being expressed as to whether James was actually Mary's son. There are suggestions that her own son died and was replaced by another baby. Some have said the portraits from the period show no resemblance between James and either of his parents. He was said to be much more like the Earl of Mar whose wife had given birth to a child at the same time, and which was said to have died. This idea, which was generally treated as nothing more than idle gossip, was given a great boost in 1830. A group of workmen were busy refurbishing the room in the Castle where Mary had given birth to James. The ancient plaster of the walls was crumbling and had to be replaced. As they were doing this, the workmen came across a recess hidden in the wall behind the plastering. Within this recess was a small, very old, oak coffin. On being opened it was found to contain the remains of a new-born child and the scraps of a silk cloth embroidered with gold thread. The cloth was extremely fragile but there was just enough of it left to see that the embroidery was of a capital 'J.' And there are those who still ask the question, was this the real James Stewart, the sixth King James of the Scots and the first King James of

England? On his deathbed his grandfather, James V, on being told that his wife had given birth to a daughter, had prophesied, 'It began wi a lass an it will end wi a lass.' This was in part a reference to Marjorie, daughter of Robert I of Scotland, known as The Bruce, through whom the Stewarts had come to the throne. He clearly thought that no female would be able to continue the line of the Stewart monarchy. He was wrong. However, it was not Mary who turned out to be the lass who was the last of the Stewart monarchs. It was in fact Queen Anne, the daughter of James VII and II, who succeeded her brother-in-law William II in 1702. By the time she herself died in 1714 Scotland had been effectively swallowed up by England, though it was nearly another 50 years before the Stewart claim to the thrones of Scotland and England stopped being the basis for political intrigue and open rebellion.

an ominous spectre

IN 1688 PRINCE WILLIAM of Orange was invited
into England by a group of Protestant lords who
were opposed to the continuing rule of James VII.
James' wife, Mary of Modena, had recently given
birth to a son who, like his father, was to be
raised as a Catholic. After the upheavals of the
1640s and 50s the English Parliament was in no
mood to accept a Catholic succession. The scars
of the Civil War ran deep and though there was
still support for James VII, the majority of the
country was united against the idea of Catholic
monarchy in a Protestant country. James fled the
country in December and in February Parliament
declared that he had abdicated his throne and
offered it jointly to William of Orange and his
wife Mary, James' eldest daughter, who was
herself a Protestant. In Scotland, which still had
its own Parliament, the Union of the Crowns
only having happened in 1603, the situation was
different, but the country was predominantly
Presbyterian and there was an equal abhorrence
of Catholicism amongst much of the population.
A Convention of the Scottish Parliament was
called in Edinburgh on 14 March 1689 and the

majority were ready to accept William and
Mary's accession to the combined thrones of
Great Britain. However, there were still many
supporters of the Stewart cause in Scotland and
one of them was the Duke of Gordon who was
commanding the Castle. For several days after
the Convention met there were widespread
disturbances in Edinburgh and the populace of
the capital rose against the better known of the
Catholic hierarchy. The cellars of several leading
Stewart loyalists, who had fled the city, were
opened up and a great deal of drink was
consumed. The situation in the city became
chaotic and there was a great deal of unease
amongst members of the garrison in the castle,
many of whom were themselves Protestants and
all in favour of the new regime.

One of the Lords who attended the Convention
was James Graham, of Claverhouse, whom James
VII had recently made Marquis of Dundee. This
famous soldier was fiercely loyal to the man he
considered his true king. Additionally, he was
inspired by the memory of his ancestor the Marquis
of Montrose who had fought for James VII's
grandfather, Charles I, whose life had ended on
the scaffold. In an incident still celebrated in song,

Claverhouse declared his loyalty to King James
before the Convention before riding out of
Edinburgh with 60 armed soldiers. As he left the
city he had a brief meeting with Gordon who came
down from the castle. Gordon thought there
might be a chance of changing the Convention's
decision but Claverhouse was adamant he was
going to raise an army for the true king, leaving
Gordon to hold the Castle till he could return.
'Where are you going to go?' asked Gordon.
'Wherever the ghost of Montrose shall lead me,'
came the ominous reply.

Gordon returned to the Castle while Montrose
and his men rode north to Dundee where, on the
Law Hill overlooking the city he raised the King's
Standard, before heading north to the Highlands to
gather fighting men for his army. The Highlanders,
predominantly Catholic, were ever keen to go
raiding, a practice their forefathers had kept up
since the Iron Age. Claverhouse left his wife and
his new-born son behind him in Glen Ogilvy in
the Sidlaw Hills, just north of Dundee. Soon after
his departure from Edinburgh a deputation from
the Convention arrived at the Castle, demanding
that Gordon hand the castle over to them. 'That
I shall not do without the explicit order of my

king,' replied Gordon, 'and my king, the one true king, is King James the Seventh of Scotland and Second of England.' And he threw some coins at the deputation telling them they should drink a health to the true king. 'I have not turned my coat,' he declared. The Convention immediately had him denounced as a traitor. All communication with him or members of his garrison was expressly forbidden and plans were put in action to besiege the castle.

The situation in the castle was precarious despite Gordon's bravado. Almost half of the troops were Presbyterians and were on the side of the Convention. Gordon was forced to let them go leaving him with a total of 86 men, among them his friend the Earl of Balcarres, and Colonel Winram who had been the Commander of the Castle till Gordon took over. They had a limited amount of gunpowder for their cannon and with their small numbers, even operating the 22 guns would be a problem. Additionally they were without a doctor, or an engineer, and the only money they had was what was in their pockets. That was of less importance than the few supplies they had, for it was unlikely they would be able to send out for food with an army surrounding

the whole of Castle Rock. For the next three
months the castle was subjected to almost
constant bombardment. Inside, the numbers of
fit men were gradually whittled down and the
diet, which was soon down to dry bread and salt
herring, was hardly sufficient to keep up their
strength. Remarkably, Gordon kept his men
fighting, turning back a whole series of direct
assaults and keeping up cannon fire against the
besieging troops, always in the expectation that
they would eventually be relieved by forces loyal
to King James. At one point Gordon asked for a
volunteer to leave the castle and find out if there
was any sign of a relief force. A man called John
Grant stepped forward and in the dead of night
was lowered over the north face of the rock and
managed to make his way through the ranks of
the Convention army. Two days later, he signalled
from a pre-arranged vantage point beyond the
besiegers. The news was bad. He had found no
word of any relief. King James was busy fighting
in Ireland and had no troops to spare to try and
relieve his tenaciously loyal men in Edinburgh.
That was at the beginning of May. Still Gordon
held out, until at last, out of food and gunpowder,
with even the wells in the castle drying up he was

forced to surrender. It was the 13 June. Having
agreed terms of surrender Gordon and the 50 men
still alive, most of them injured and all of them
stick-thin, marched out of the castle. He had been
promised they would all be set free, but Winram
and Gordon were both imprisoned and the
bedraggled survivors were abused and assaulted
by the citizens of Edinburgh. Gordon, as befitted
an aristocrat, was put under house arrest in his
home in Blair's Close, and soon given parole.
Winram and Balcarres were locked back up in
the Castle they had fought so hard to defend.

As they lay in their cells, the Government
troops began repairing the extensive damage that
had been done during the siege. Then something
happened that Balcarres would talk about for the
rest of his life. He was lying on his bed during
the day on 27 July. As with most prisoners, time
lay heavy on his hands and he was dozing with
the curtains, a standard fixture of beds in those
days, drawn shut. Suddenly, without a sound, a
hand drew back the curtains and Balcarres was
astonished to see John Graham standing there
fully dressed with his flowing wig, cocked hat,
shining breastplate and pistols at his side.
Claverhouse stood looking down at him, with a

gloomy countenance. The hairs on the back of
Balcarres' neck rose and his blood turned cold as
he realised that he could see the far end of the
cell through Claverhouse's body. The spectre
looked at him with a look of great sorrow,
walked over to the mantelpiece at the fireplace
and gazed into the ashes. Then the ghost turned
and left the chamber, without having made a
sound. Balcarres was deeply upset but it was not
till the following day that news came from the
north that explained this eerie visit. Claverhouse
had indeed gathered a Highland army and had
won a battle against the Government forces
under General Mackay just north of the Pass of
Killiecrankie, in Perthshire. Although
outnumbered two to one, such was the ferocity
of the Highlanders' attack, that they had routed
the regular troops of the British Army. However,
close to the end of the battle, Claverhouse himself
had been shot from his horse as he watched his
men win their great battle. He was dead as he hit
the ground, and with his passing went all hope of
victory for the Jacobite forces. His Highland army
returned to their homes, many of them content
with the booty they had gathered on their brief
campaign, and many of the others, including

most of Claverhouse's officers, left for the Continent. The courage and sacrifice of the tiny garrison who had held out in Edinburgh Castle for all those months had been in vain.

a dashing hero

IN 1715 THE WIDESPREAD plotting to bring back
the Stewart kings erupted into open rebellion.
The Earl of Mar, who until a few years before
had been working for the British Government,
had been spurned by Queen Anne and switched
to the Jacobite cause. He was now intent on
bringing back James VIII to rule both Scotland
and England. There was widespread support for
the Jacobite cause in Scotland, partly because of
the resentment against the Act of Union, which
was felt to have been corruptly foisted on the
Scots. However, in John, Earl of Mar, the
Jacobite cause had a leader whose military and
organisational skills were not up to the job. His
nickname was Bobbin John, because he was
thought to be bobbing around from one position
to another. In truth he had been the British
Government's leading authority in Scotland until,
falling out of favour he had decided to become a
Jacobite.

While Bobbin John's spectacular ineptitude
ensured the eventual failure of the Rising there
were many brave and talented men who flocked
to the cause of 'the King over the Water'. One of

these was David Thriepland of Fingask, in the Carse of Gowrie on the north bank of the river Tay. Like many young men of the time David was keen for adventure as well as being committed to the Jacobite cause, and he found himself under the command of Mackintosh of Borlum, an experienced and capable soldier. Once Mar had raised his army and gathered his troops together at Perth it was decided that help should be sent to the Jacobites in the north of England. It was believed that, if they were given sufficient military support, the Catholics and many Episcopalians in the north of England would rally to the Jacobite cause, making it much easier to invade England, defeat the British army and restore the Stewart monarchy.

Borlum was given about 2,000 men for the job, but first he had to make his way through Scotland. This was problematic, for the Duke of Argyll had a considerable number of troops at Stirling and it was felt that rather than fighting their way through it would be better if Borlum's troops, mainly Highlanders, avoided Argyll's troops. This was hardly an easy task as the British Navy had three men-o-war patrolling the Firth of Forth with the express aim of preventing any shipment of troops south to the Lothians and beyond. Borlum, however, was up to the job. He split his men into two groups. The smaller group of around 500 were sent to Burntisland to make it look like they were going to embark on a crossing of the firth. Borlum took the rest of his troops, with Thriepland among them, to the ports of the East Neuk of Fife, Crail, Elie and Pittenweem. All the fishing boats and other vessels in the area were gathered into these small ports. Pausing only to build defensive earth banks for their limited number of cannon, the troops in Burntisland sent out a handful of boats. Immediately the English ships sailed up the Firth and began firing on the boats and the men on shore. The boats immediately returned to Burntisland and the batteries on shore began to exchange fire with the three ships. Borlum's plan was simple. He wanted to keep the English ships at Burntisland till the tide turned. The wind had been blowing from the east for several days and as long as it didn't turn, the English ships would be unable to tack east from Burntisland once the tide was on the turn.

So at dawn the first boats set out from the East Neuk ports. The English were soon aware of what was happening and the three captains used all their seamanship to try to make their way towards the fleet of small boats ferrying the Highlanders across to the Lothians. It took several hours for the first boats to cross and soon the main body of the Jacobite army was safely landed on the south side of the river. However, by the time most of them had landed and moved inshore away from any possible bombardment from the English ships, the tide turned. The English ships made good speed towards the handful of boats still crossing. Some of the boats headed for the Isle of May, where they were undisturbed and managed to row back to Fife the following day. However two boats were still in the open water, and David Thriepland was in one of them. As the battle ships approached, the occupants of the boats realised they had no choice but to surrender. If they attempted to fight or flee they would simply be blown out of the water. They didn't have a chance.

So they were all captured. At once, the ship which had taken them turned for the port of Leith, which was still in the hands of British troops. Here David and his companions were locked in the Tolbooth under armed guard. His great

adventure seemed to have failed at the very start.
After a night in the stinking cells of Leith Tolbooth,
David was delighted when Borlum's men took Leith
with hardly a fight and released their comrades.
Although the plan was to head directly to England,
it was necessary to find out where the British
Army troops were. The small garrison that had
held Leith were now in the same place David and
his companions had spent the night but Borlum
was aware that there was the garrison at Edinburgh
and that Argyll might well have sent more troops
from Stirling. There was also the possibility that
other troops were heading north from England.
As he gathered stores and ammunition for his
journey south Borlum kept sending out patrols
towards Edinburgh. Some of these fought
skirmishes with Argyll's men but there was no
major incident. After a couple of days when
preparations for the march south were well
advanced, David Thriepland went out on one of
these patrols. He had half a dozen men with him
and was riding towards the capital when he
found himself surrounded by a force of nearly a
hundred Redcoats. Resistance was pointless and
yet again he found himself a prisoner. This time
he was taken to the Tolbooth in Edinburgh, but

a day or so later was transferred to Edinburgh
Castle, a totally different scenario from being
locked up in the old Tolbooth at Leith. Now he
was incarcerated in the most impregnable
fortress in the whole of Scotland. A few days
after being locked in the castle he heard that
Borlum and the rest of his companions had gone
south to England. There they fought well, but
due to the pathetic leadership that always seemed
to dog the Jacobite cause they were eventually
compelled to surrender.

Meanwhile, in the Castle David realised there
was no chance of a further rescue. Borlum had
gone south and the rest of Mar's army was still
up north in Perth as far as he knew. If he were to
get out he would have to do it himself. Luckily
he had been put into a room with half a dozen
other prisoners, high up in the Castle, overlooking
a path round the Castle Rock. As the path was
40 or 50 feet below where they were imprisoned,
the officers of the guard had seen no need to bar
the windows. The rock below them was absolutely
perpendicular and the path was only a few feet
wide, having another extensive, steep drop on its
other side. The commander of the troops on the
castle thought that anyone attempting to climb

down it would simply fall to their deaths, or at least be seriously injured. Now it was common practice for some of the local people to take a stroll around Castle Rock in the evening and such activity was an established part of the capital's social scene. Being the son of a wealthy landowner David had often been in Edinburgh and on more than a few occasions he had taken just such a stroll himself. One day while looking down from his window he spotted a group of four young ladies coming along the path. He recognised them from a couple of social occasions the previous year and was certain that two of them at least were from a Jacobite family. Running quickly to the cell door he looked to see if there were any guards about. There were none. At once he went back to the window and leaning out as far as he could he gently called to the young ladies as they passed below the window.

'Hello Margaret, hello Marjorie,' he called out as quietly as he could.

The two sisters looked up on hearing their names. They saw a young man leaning out of a window above them.

'Who is it?' Marjorie asked her elder sister.

'I'm not sure,' said Margaret, then she

gasped. 'It's Davie Thriepland! I'd heard he had been captured.'

'Hello Davie,' she said loudly, waving her hand.

Terrified that the guards might hear but delighted that the girls had reacted, he held a finger to his lips and said 'Wheesht.' At once Margaret understood and nodded her head. Marjorie was giggling as she explained to the other two that this was David Thriepland, a young man who was considered a bit of a catch in Edinburgh society. David waved the girls to come forward till they were right under the window. He looked around, luckily there was nobody else on that part of the path for the moment but he would have to be quick. He realised that these giggling lassies were his only hope. Then he saw that Margaret was shushing the others and as she looked up at him he could see that she at least understood the seriousness of the situation. Keeping his voice as quiet as he could he said, 'Tonight, can you bring blankets. At least ten?' Margaret looked quizzically at him. Quickly he mimed tearing them up and tying them together. The other three girls began giggling again and he could see that Margaret hadn't cottoned on to what he meant. Again he mimed tearing up the blankets and tying them together. Suddenly Margaret smiled. She understood. She nodded vigorously and mouthed, 'What time?' He held up nine fingers. Again she nodded and then turned to her sister and the others and said, 'Let's go, now.'

As the four young ladies headed off along the path a middle-aged couple came into sight around the corner of the castle wall. He had been lucky, there hadn't been moment to spare. He lay back against the wall inside his cell and realised that his heart was racing. His companions were all looking at him. He hadn't said anything to them before but now he quickly explained. He had managed to steal a length of strong cord when they had been allowed out on the battlements a week earlier. He had already rejected the idea of using the blankets that were in the cell to make a rope, they were cheap and badly made of thin cloth. He had taken the cord with the vague hope that something could be done to make an escape attempt. But it hadn't been until he saw Margaret and Marjorie that the plan had formed in his head. He outlined his idea. It was dangerous but they were all anxious to break out and return to the Jacobite forces. This might be their only chance. 'Can you trust the lassies?' asked Callum MacKenzie, a Highlander from Moidart. 'I think so. We'll just have to wait and see,' David replied. The next few hours seemed to last an eternity. At last night fell. David paced up and down the cell bumping into his companions sitting along the walls. His heart was pounding as nine o'clock approached and he kept looking out into the dark. There was no moon but it was cloudless night and by the light of the stars he could just make out the path where it curved round the corner of the castle wall. He chewed his lip. Would the girls come back? Would they have managed to get blankets? Would anybody see them and get suspicious? His thoughts were racing.

Suddenly he saw a shadow come round the path then another, and another. As the figures stopped below the window he saw that three of the girls had returned and each of them was carrying four blankets. How they had managed to come up from the High Street and round the path without being seen he could not imagine. Maybe they had brought them up one at a time earlier. Quickly he lowered the cord and Margaret tied it round the first blanket. He hoisted it up, untied it and passed it back to his companions.

As they began to tear it into strips he lowered the cord again. The action was repeated till at last all of the blankets were in the cell. As soon as the last blanket was in the girls waved and turned to go. Their presence was a danger if anyone came round the path, which was unlikely at this hour, but they could be spotted by a sentry on the battlements. As they turned Margaret looked over her shoulder. In the dark he couldn't make out if she was smiling but he took the opportunity to blow her a kiss. She waved back then headed off. Thriepland realised how much he owed this brave lass and there and then made a vow to himself that if the chance came he would make a point of visiting her and thanking her properly. She was a fine looking lass too but there were more pressing matters to think of than the possibility of future romance. It took the five men about half an hour to tear up the blankets and make a strong rope. Then they tied one end of it to the frame of one of the rough wooden beds in the cell and lowered it out of the window. 'Right lads,' said David with a smile. 'Let's go.' One by one, as quietly as they could, the five young men slid down the rope to the path below. Once they were all down David led them along the path to the west and a few minutes later they were off Castle Rock and heading through fields towards the Haymarket. Keeping in the shadows they made their way through the scattered houses and out towards Corstorphine, keeping their eyes open for red-coated soldiers. They were free! They stopped at an inn just past Corstorphine where one of them knew the proprietor was a staunch Jacobite, and after a meal and a good night's sleep headed off via Stirling and on to rejoin the Jacobite army at Perth. They had managed to escape from Scotland's most famous castle, a feat that was talked about for generations.

a major folly

IN 1745 THE WHOLE country was in a ferment. Prince Charlie had landed at Glenfinnan and raised an army to try to regain the thrones of Scotland and England for the Stewarts. Throughout the Highlands, and most of the north-east, there was strong support for the Jacobite cause and in most parts of the country considerable numbers of the population were also ready to support the Stewarts. The capital city was no exception, with the population being pretty evenly divided between the Jacobites and the Hanoverians, as the supporters of the incoming German monarchy were called. There was a strong religious element to people's loyalties, with the Scottish Catholics and Episcopalians securely in the Stewart camp while many Presbyterians, and particularly their ministers, tended to be supporters of the Government, whom they saw as protectors against the possibility of a return to Catholic kings. The situation, however, was complicated by the ongoing resentment of English power, which had never disappeared from Scottish society, and in particular the taverns of Edinburgh. For many Scots the idea of having the Stewarts back was as much to do with being Scottish as anything specific, like religion or politics. There had been constant plotting and fantasising in Edinburgh's many taverns ever since the Battle of Killiecrankie, back in 1689. It was a common sight to see one of a company of drinkers either passing a water jug over glasses of whisky or waving glasses of wine over the water jug as a surreptitious salute to 'the King over the Water', Prince Charlie's father and, according to the Jacobites, James VIII of Scotland and III of the United Kingdom.

At this period in time drinking was something of a national sport in Scotland and nowhere more so than in Edinburgh. People from all levels of society drank a fearsome amount and the streets at night were the scene for many a judge and carter being carried home after a night's steady drinking in the city's taverns. Most social activity took place in the taverns, inns, and clubs and with the water supply being none too clean, people tended to drink at all times of the day. The widespread drunkenness was referred to as 'conviviality' and very few activities, from High Court trials to the selling of goods, took place without some drink being involved. In fact, back then people drank booze like we drink tea or coffee today and nobody thought anything about it. This penchant for a glass or two gave rise to one of the sillier incidents that took place at Edinburgh Castle.

It was September in 1746 and the Jacobites were intent on taking Edinburgh Castle, garrisoned as it was by Government troops. Apart from its strategic value it was the most high profile military establishment in the country and its capture would be a great propaganda victory. Also, the castle held a considerable amount of arms and ammunition and a large amount of cash, in gold. Lord Drummond was given the task of organising the capture of the castle. The widespread support for the Jacobite cause included many Scots, and some Englishmen, serving in the British Army. One of these was Ensign Thomas Arthur who was posted at the castle that September, and he was contacted by Drummond and given the job of organising a surprise nighttime attack. On the evening of 6 September, Arthur approached James Thomson, one of the private soldiers under his command, whom he suspected might be sympathetic. He asked Thomson to meet him the following day at his lodgings in a house in the Canongate. Once

Thomson had agreed the Ensign then approached Corporal John Holland, asking him to join them next day. On the 7th the two soldiers were on their way to the Canongate when they were met in the street by Ensign Thomas and taken to a nearby house in the High Street. Now both the young soldiers realised that they were going to be asked to do something that would probably be treasonous, but were ready to do their bit for the cause.

Once they were indoors, Thomas asked Thomson to come into another room with him. When they were alone the Ensign came straight to the point, 'Now Thomson,' he said, 'I believe you feel a loyalty to the cause I hold deep in my heart, as do all true Scots. Are you one of us?'

'What exactly do you mean, sir,' replied Thomson cautiously.

'Come on, man, you know exactly what I mean. Do you support the cause of the true king, the King over the Water, or do ye not?'

Thomson noticed that as he spoke, the young officer had his hand clasped firmly on the butt of the pistol holstered at his belt.

'Och aye sir, I do support the cause,' Thomson hurriedly said.

'That's grand. Now we have a plan to take over the castle and we need your help. It should all go as we intend and none of your comrades need be hurt.' He then added, 'we will of course make it worth your while my man. How would you like a hundred guineas for your help?' Thomson had never even seen such a sum of money and the thought of being rich as well as helping the cause seemed very attractive.

'It would be an honour sir tae help the prince in onie way I can, whit have I to do?' he replied. He was then given instructions to turn up at another house the following evening and to bring Private William Ainslie, another of the regular sentinels, with him. Thomson was then dismissed but before leaving, the Ensign gave him 40 shillings as a sign of his good faith. The next night he and Ainslie turned up at the house in Weir's Land where they were met by Arthur and a group of other men, including Charles Forbes of Brux in Aberdeenshire, and the owner of the house, a local Catholic called Pringle. Forbes had been in exile with the Prince and was excited at the chance of seeing some action. As the plans were finalised, over a few glasses of claret, the two soldiers were pleasantly surprised to learn that not only would they earn themselves a hundred guineas each, but once the castle was taken they would be commissioned as lieutenants in the Jacobite army.

The following evening all three of the soldiers, privates Ainslie and Thomson and Corporal Holland were scheduled to be on duty on the Castle battlements. They were to wait for nine o'clock, when a signal would sound from the rock below where they were due to be on duty. While Holland acted as lookout, the other two were to take out a weighted rope, supplied earlier by Ensign Arthur, and lower it down the cliff to where a band of men would be waiting with ladders. The sentries were to haul up the first ladder, allowing the attackers to climb up to the battlements and bring up the rest of their party behind them. Under cover of darkness it seemed an easy task and once they were all on the battlements they would silently spread out through the castle, disarm the rest of the sentries and neutralise the off-duty soldiers, most of whom would be asleep in their quarters. They did not anticipate much difficulty in gaining control of the castle, after which they could lock up the British troops in the cells deep in the Castle Rock.

They could then move to the next stage of the plan, which was to fire off a series of cannons to acquaint the Jacobite troops waiting outside the city to the west, with the fact that the castle had been taken. These troops would also start a series of cannon fire across the country to spread the word that Scotland's most famous castle had been taken for the Jacobite cause.

Hiding the weighted rope below his tunic, Thomson left with Ainslie and the two soldiers went in customary fashion to a nearby tavern for a drink before they went on duty. They were not the only ones, and before the sentries even went on duty the plan was already compromised. The day before, Ensign Arthur had gone to visit his brother who worked as a doctor in the town. However, all did not go as planned. The young officer was so excited about the contribution he was about to make for the Jacobite cause that he not help telling his brother. Sadly his brother, who was not so much of a Jacobite as the Ensign, was a bit distracted by his brother's intended actions. His wife, who was no Jacobite, being the daughter of a Presbyterian minister who was staunchly Hanoverian, asked him what was wrong and he told her. Although she was well aware that she might be leading her brother-in-law to the gallows on a charge of treason, she felt it was her Christian duty to inform the authorities. However, she felt it would be better to do so anonymously. Accordingly a short while later a note was delivered to the home of the Lord Justice Clerk, Sir Adam Cockburn of Ormiston. Now ever since the Prince had landed there had been constant rumours and supposed inside information about Jacobite attacks on the capital city and the Castle, and Cockburn thought this as unlikely to be true as any of the others he had received. However, he was a man who held to the old adage – better safe than sorry – and he passed the note on to Lieutenant-Colonel Stewart, the officer commanding the Castle garrison. He also passed on news of the warning to the Lord Provost, urging him to make sure the Town Guard was extra vigilant that night. The Town Guard was a sort of local police force who patrolled the dark streets of Edinburgh at night to keep law and order.

By the time they started their shifts the young men were both extremely nervous and Holland kept coming along to ask if anything had happened. Another hour passed. All three of them were beginning to suspect that nothing was going to happen that night, but just after eleven three owl hoots sounded from below the battlements. This was the agreed signal. Looking out over the battlements into the dark, Thomson could just make out indistinct movements. He could hear some scuffling. Leaning over the rampart, he whispered, 'Who's there?'

'Wheesht, man, it's me, Ensign Arthur,' came the reply. 'Drop the cord man and keep quiet, there's a good lad.'

Thomson was already feeling anxious and realised that Ensign Arthur sounded quite drunk, he was making quite a bit of noise himself telling his comrades on the rock to be quiet. It was obvious what had happened. Arthur and his companions had spent the earlier part of the night in one tavern or another, celebrating the great victory they were about to have. A combination of excitement and nerves, mixed with the habits of conviviality had resulted in an assault party attempting to take Scotland's greatest castle whilst drunk. While the sentries on the ramparts had been sweating with worry, the rest of the conspirators had been toasting the King over the Water with round after round of drinks. Things were now moving ahead and Thomson carefully lowered the rope, feeling a tug as it was caught by the men below. A minute or so later there were two tugs on the rope, this was the signal to start pulling up the first ladder. As quietly as they could the two sentries got a grip on the rope and began hauling. They had barely started when Corporal Holland came running up. 'Quick, lads. Lieutenant Lindsay is coming on his rounds. Let go of that rope!' Both let go of the ladder, which slid down the rock. As it fell among the group below there was burst of drunken shouting. Just then Lindsay came running up to the sentries.

'What's happening, Corporal?' He demanded, a cocked pistol in his hand.

'I think there might be someone on the rock below, sir,' replied Holland.

'Probably damned Jacobites,' Lindsay said. 'Fire freely at any sound you hear.'

At once the three sentries levelled their guns down into the darkness and fired their muskets, taking care to aim away from the rock-face. A burst of noise came from below, and just after the first shot the alarm was sounded. Immediately the rest of the guards came running, while the off-duty troops were roused from their beds and

Lieutenant-Colonel Stewart was informed of the attack. Soon, the battlements above where the attack was set were manned by more than two dozen soldiers. Lindsay organised another group of about 20 men to head out of the castle with torches to see what was happening on the rock below. Thomson and some of the others were firing off occasional shots but there was no answering fire from below. The party outside the gates spread out down the rock and carefully headed for the spot below Ainslie and the others. Once they were directly below they found two men sprawled on a ledge on the rock, both almost comatose with drink. There was no sign of any others. One of them was a Catholic priest and the other was a young stable lad called Graham. He worked for Forbes of Brux and had been drawn into the plot with the promise of riches and glory. There was the sound of running feet as the Town Guard came up to the castle to join the soldiers looking at the result of the glorious attack on Edinburgh Castle.

It didn't take Lieutenant Lindsay long to realise that the rope attached to one of the ladders had to have been dropped from above. Clearly Ainslie and Thomson were in on the plot and probably Holland too. All three were immediately arrested and taken to the cells. A party was organised to scout round the whole area around the base of Castle Rock. There was no sign of anybody else. In the morning the shortcomings of the attack were all too plain to see. The ladders found on the rock below the ramparts were too short for the job, even if they hadn't been discovered, the drunken party of Jacobites would have had problems scaling the battlements. A second group of attackers, who did have longer ladders, had been on their way round Castle Rock from the Norloch when they heard the shots. They had dropped their equipment and fled into the night, just like the majority of Ensign Thomas's party. Stewart realised that despite the amateurish nature of the attempt, it could well have succeeded and sent a message to Lord Islay, the Duke of Argyll's brother, asking for reinforcements. Before nightfall of the following day a contingent of 60 well-armed troops arrived from the West to bolster the garrison.

After a substantial investigation it was clear that Ainslie, Thompson and Holland were all guilty of a raft of charges, the most serious of course being treason, a capital offence. Private

Ainslie was hanged on a gallows erected on the battlements of the Castle on the precise spot where the conspirators had intended climbing the wall. For weeks after, his body swung in the wind over the battlements. Surprisingly, his companions, Thompson and Holland, were not hanged, but were sentenced to be flogged, though that particular form of punishment was truly horrendous and often killed those subjected to it. In this case both survived to serve long sentences. Other than the stable lad, Graham, and the Catholic priest, the conspirators had escaped. The Government were of course delighted that the attempted seizure of the castle failed, but we can only look back and wonder at the utter stupidity and carelessness of the men selected by Lord Drummond on behalf of his exiled king to attack the most important fortress in Scotland. Men who celebrated victory before the battle was joined, falling prey to the conviviality of Scotland's capital city.

escape at any cost

IN THE AFTERMATH OF the Battle of Culloden in April 1746 there was a great deal of brutality throughout the Highlands of Scotland. The Duke of Cumberland deliberately encouraged the destruction of Highland homes and the brutal mistreatment of the majority of the local people, often including those who had nothing to do with the Jacobite cause and some of whom were staunch government supporters. To Cumberland, the King's second son, and most of his officers, these Highlanders were nothing but savages, subhuman creatures from another world. Despite the loyalty of many Scots even the Lowland towns were all garrisoned by troops and the country was effectively under a military occupation. Many prisoners were allowed to die of their injuries and the death toll on the filthy and disease ridden prison hulks in the River Thames was considerable. However, not all Jacobite prisoners had cause to curse their fate. Thomas Ogilvy, from Eastmiln in Glenisla, had been out in the '45 as a Captain in the regiment raised by his distant cousin David, Lord Ogilvy. In the period after the regiment was disbanded at the head of

Glen Clova a couple of weeks after Culloden, he had decided to return home. For some reason he thought he might be able to return to his old life as a tenant farmer but in truth, there was little chance of that. Cumberland's intent was to hunt down and capture as many of the Jacobite traitors as could be found. A contingent of Hessian troops from Germany were sent to Cortachy Castle in Angus to scour the area for rebels and arrest and imprison all those who had been active in the Jacobite cause. While the vast majority of the population of Angus and Perthshire were supporters of the Stewarts and would never inform on any of the Jacobite soldiers, there were quite a number of people who strongly supported the Government, particularly amongst the Presbyterian ministry, who were virulently opposed to the Stewarts and what they saw as their readiness to restore the Catholic faith.

With the Hessian troops stationed at the Ogilvies' ancestral home at Cortachy it was only a matter of time before word was sent to the commander of the troops at Cortachy that here was one of the rebels blatantly acting as if nothing untoward had happened at all. It was a simple matter to send word to the garrison in

Glenisla to arrest him, and given that he was a
man of some standing in his local community, he
was ordered to be taken to Edinburgh for trial.
His trial, like most of those in Scotland at the
time, was a farce and the verdict was a foregone
conclusion. Now Thomas realised that his bold
plan of returning to his home in the hills had
been foolish indeed. Many of his comrades had
been executed, some by the brutal method of
being hung, drawn and quartered, a positively
sadistic sentence that was still the official fate for
all those convicted of High Treason under
English law. The niceties of the differences
between the law in Scotland and England were
ignored, with no complaints from the Scottish
bench. Although he feared being hanged,
Thomas was actually more worried about being
sent out to the Colonies. Hundreds of imprisoned
Jacobites were in fact sent abroad, most without
trial, to the sugar plantations of Jamaica. They
were told they would save their lives if they agreed
to sign up with the traders gathering workers for
the plantations. In fact they were nothing but
slaves and many of them died under the blistering
hot sun of the West Indies. A few managed to
escape to the American colonies but there were

few, if any, who ever saw their beloved Scotland again.

Thomas however was lucky, after a fashion. He was sentenced neither to death nor transportation. He was simply imprisoned in Edinburgh Castle itself. He was in good company, for alongside him there were the Earl of Kellie, MacDonald of Kingsburgh, MacDonald of Glengarry, Lady Strathallan and the redoubtable Lady Ogilvy. Within a year or so many of the Jacobite prisoners were granted indemnity and released. But for Thomas, having served as an officer in the Jacobite army, and thus being guilty of treason, there was no hope of release. As a relatively humble tenant farmer he had no real money or rich connections with which to try to influence the government. Bribing the guards was equally impossible and though he knew that the Earl of Airlie himself would have helped, his hands were tied because of the role his son had played in the Rebellion. Ogilvy began to think he would never see his beloved Strathisla again. He had been sentenced to life and it looked as if he might have to serve the full sentence. Looking out from the battlements of the Castle on the few hours he was allowed out of his cell the sight of the distant hills to the north brought a pain to his heart. Far off in the distance on clear days he could see the conical peak of Schiehallion, over 60 miles away and whenever he saw it his thoughts turned to the hills and straths of his home in Glen Isla, 30 miles to the east of the great mountain.

Security at the Castle was tight, but Thomas decided that he had to try to escape. The thought of spending the rest of his life in prison was too much. It would be dangerous trying to break out of the castle and go down the sheer rock surrounding it. He checked out the gate but there was no possibility of getting out that way, it would have to be down the rock. However, he reasoned that if he fell and was killed it would still be a preferable option to a life cooped up in a stinking cell, with only a few hours of fresh air every few days. He also felt that being able to see the mountains would just increase his sorrow and make the situation even worse. As the years passed he became obsessed with escaping. The fact that David Thriepland and his companions had managed to escape from the Castle 30 years earlier kept him going. He just knew an opportunity would present itself. He had managed to hide a knife a guard left with his food one day and over the next few weeks, he carefully familiarised himself with the corridors leading up to the doors out on to the battlements. However his opportunity did not come soon.

In the spring of 1751 on one of his permitted walks around the battlements, which had become more frequent as time passed, Thomas saw a net bundled up behind a pile of shot beside one of the cannons pointing over the battlements to the north. It had been used to carry cannonballs up to the castle in the back of a cart and it appeared it might be at least 30 feet long once unrolled. Such was his excitement at the possibility of escape he had no doubt that it would get him down to a level where he could use his climbing skills to get down the rest of the way, this was his chance. While the guard on duty was looking the other way he quickly moved to the net and bundled it under his coat. He walked hunched over as if against the wind blowing hard across Castle Rock till he was escorted back to his cell. The guard hadn't noticed anything. He rolled out the net, and sure enough it was about 30 feet long. But would that be enough? Now if he could just get out of his cell after dark he could tie one end of the net to the cannon and throw the other end of

it over the battlements and could then let himself
down onto the rock. He had been used to climbing
mountains since he was barely able to walk.
Getting down Castle Rock even in the dark should
be within the capabilities of a mountain man like
himself. He had noticed that the wood around
the lock on his door was rotting away and had
been toying with the idea of prising it loose with
the knife he had hidden. Now there was good
reason to do it.

The following morning the sun rose on a clear,
bright day. One of the sentries making his early
morning rounds noticed the net hanging over the
battlements. He peered over but could see nothing.
At once he ran to the officer of the watch. The
office immediately ordered a check on the
prisoners in their cells and ordered half-a-dozen-
men to head out to check below where the net
had been flung over the castle wall. It was only a
matter of minutes before word came that the
prisoner, Thomas Ogilvy, was missing from his
cell. The Captain began to shout at the sentry
before him. How had a net been left lying about?
Someone would pay for this. He was still
remonstrating about carelessness and slipshod
behaviour when the Corporal in charge of the

search party returned. Thomas had got free from his cell, but he had not got far. The patrol had found his crippled body, smashed almost beyond recognition at the floor of Castle Rock. Thomas's climbing skills had done him little good. The once powerful and fit mountaineer had had his strength sapped by years of lousy food and little exercise in the prison of Edinburgh Castle. Even a younger, fitter Thomas might well have found climbing down the sheer face of the rock, in darkness, too much. Never again, in this life at least, would Thomas Ogilvy walk through the mountains of his beloved Glen Isla.

Lady Ogilvy's adventures

AFTER THE ABORTIVE ATTEMPT at capturing the Castle in 1745 many Jacobites ended up seeing the inside of the Castle, as prisoners. One of them was a woman known for her beauty, but who proved that when it came to courage she was the match of any man. She was Margaret Johnstone of Auchterhouse, near Dundee, who had married David, the eldest son of Lord Ogilvy, the Earl of Airlie and one of the leading officers in Prince Charlie's Jacobite army. After the fateful final battle at Culloden on 16 April 1746, Lady Margaret, who had been at the battlefield holding a spare horse for her husband, fled to Inverness ahead of the triumphant red-coated soldiers of the British army. This was not the first time she had been on a battlefield and she had already had a series of adventures with the Jacobite army, barely managing to escape from the government troops at Stirling as the Jacobite army headed north. Previous to that, her coach had been rumoured to be carrying a large amount of cash for the Prince himself, not the

last time Margaret would be mistaken for
Charles Edward Stewart. Now though, the battle
was over, the cause was lost, at least for now,
and escape was the order of the day. As a leading
Jacobite David was high on the list of the
Government's most wanted and Lady Margaret
was also on the list. She was seen as a true
heroine by the Jacobites and although the Earl of
Airlie had kept out of the rising, the family thus
hedging their bets, the Ogilvies were considered
major targets. Nothing could be done against the
Earl himself but the rest of his family were fair
game, the authorities being well aware of just
how many of the leading families in Scotland
were used to playing both sides.

Lady Ogilvy was not only an outstanding
beauty but, as her actions showed, she was a
woman of remarkable strength of character. She
was one of the belles of the ball at Prince Charles
Edward Stuart's short-lived court in Edinburgh and
accompanied the Jacobite Army on its ill-fated
foray into England. During the retreat from
Derby she was sent ahead of the main body of
troops in a coach with a substantial mounted
escort. Somehow a rumour started that the coach
in fact contained the Prince and a great deal of

gold. This was probably the cause of the attack on the coach that took place at Lancaster in which three people were killed but the assailants, not government troops, were driven off and Margaret was unharmed. Now at this time both the government and the Jacobites had extensive intelligence networks throughout England and Scotland and on their way north Lady Ogilvy's party heard that there was another ambush planned near Perth. It seems that someone with the party was sending information ahead of them, so she returned to the main body of the army.

On their way north in January 1746 the Jacobite army laid siege to Stirling Castle. Her husband being off with the troops, Lady Ogilvy was billeted in a local inn. A British army, led by General Henry Hawley, was approaching from the south. Most of the Jacobite army set off to meet the approaching forces and had their last victory, such as it was, at the Battle of Falkirk on the 17th. After this they headed north, picking up the troops besieging the castle as they went. Nobody, however, told Lady Ogilvy what was happening, and the following morning she awoke at the inn to find the town of Stirling filling up with Hawley's troops. They had re-formed after the Battle of Falkirk and having been reinforced with more troops, were following the Jacobite Army. Her coach was outside the inn, and from her bed she could hear the sound of a troop of government soldiers surrounding her coach. As quick thinking as she was brave, she moved quickly and headed out of the back of the inn and along the road out of town. She had dressed herself in the spare clothes of her maid, leaving her own rich dresses hidden under a bed. Luckily she also had some money, and soon she and her maid managed to get themselves horses and rode off after the army. We can imagine the words she had with her husband for abandoning her to the not-so-tender mercies of the Government troops.

On the 16 April 1746 she was on Drummosie Moor, once more holding a spare horse for her husband, when the unfortunate tactics of the Prince and his advisers led the Jacobites into the hellish slaughter of Culloden. Once the battle was lost she headed for a friend's house not far away, but was soon identified and captured. Probably because of her status she was not subjected to the brutality that so many Scots women underwent at the hands of the Government forces, but was sent to the prison in Inverness. Prisons in those days were grim places. While there, she heard the uplifting news that her husband had managed to escape to the Continent. After two months in Inverness she was escorted to Edinburgh Castle, where she would at least be more comfortable. As a notable aristocrat and one who had played such an important role at the Prince's court, the Government intended making an example of her. They didn't, however, allow for her courage and intelligence. While she was locked up in Edinburgh Castle, Lady Ogilvy was visited regularly by her sister, Barbara, who lived in Edinburgh. Barbara had arranged for a local woman to handle Lady Ogilvy's laundry and soon she was a regular sight going back and forth from the castle. She had an assistant, a young lass who carried the laundry up to the Castle Gate for her but was not allowed in. The laundress herself was an older woman who had been born with a twisted back and walked with a very pronounced limp. Once, after delivering the clean laundry, she was about to leave the cell when Lady Ogilvy spoke.

'You have a strange way of walking, would you mind if I tried to walk the same way?' She said with a smile.

'Well, if it pleases your Ladyship, I can see no

harm in it,' replied the bemused laundress, thinking to herself, 'It's right enough what they say about the nobility, they are gey queer.' So over the next few visits Lady Ogilvy was coached in how to limp like the laundress. She then broached her plan to the laundress and asked her to smuggle in a spare set of her own clothes amongst the laundry, over the next week.

In the evening a day or so later, when the warden came to Lady Ogilvy's cell with a servant carrying her evening meal, he met Barbara at the door of her sister's quarters.

'I am sorry,' she said. 'My sister is unwell. She does not want any food. If you don't mind I will stay here tonight and keep her company. She really isn't well at all.'

The warden agreed to let her stay and Barbara went back into the cell and he heard her whispering to her sister. Barbara then came back to the cell door and quietly wished the warden a good night. In the morning when her breakfast was brought, Barbara said she had had a bad night but had fallen asleep and seemed to be more peaceful now. It wasn't until the following day, a Monday, that the truth was discovered. The guards on the gate of the Castle had not noticed that two limping maids had gone down the hill on the Saturday evening, and why should they? It had been carefully arranged that Lady Ogilvy, dressed in the laundress's clothes and feigning her limp and hunched way of walking, would go out of the Castle first, and the old woman would follow after the guard on the gate was changed. Barbara had left early the following morning, and as she was a regular visitor none of the guards had noticed anything strange.

Lady Ogilvy had simply pulled the shawl over her head, lifted the laundry basket and hobbled her way down to the gate to join the young lass outside the castle gate. None of the guards paid any attention to the crippled figure passing by them and once the pair of them were clear of the Castle they turned into one of the many wynds leading off the High Street and disappeared from view. The young lass was a bit taken aback at her mistress's silence as she was normally keen to chat about her visits to Lady Ogilvy. You can imagine her surprise when once they were a fair distance from the castle the old crooked lady whipped off her shawl and stood up, revealing herself to be a graceful and beautiful young woman. She took the young lass's hand, pressed some silver coins into it and said, 'Now you will not tell anyone of this, will you? Your mistress said you were a fine lass and that I can count on you.' The lassie could only nod agreement, being totally lost for words. Lady Ogilvy smiled at her companion, winked broadly, and ran off. She then made her way down the Royal Mile to a friend's house in Abbey Hill where a set of men's clothing and a horse was waiting for her, as was her personal maid. Lingering only long enough to say farewell to her faithful friends, the pair of them set off south. They did not take the road to London where the chance of being recognised and arrested were considerable, as they saw no point in exchanging the confines of Edinburgh Castle for Tower Hill. Instead they made their way, by back roads whenever possible, to Hull, where there was a ship waiting to take them on to Rotterdam. At last she and her maid got on board the ship that was to take them to safety on the Continent.

But even this was not the end of her adventures. A rumour sprang up that the gentleman who had boarded the ship was in fact Prince Charlie himself. A search party of soldiers was sent for and came on board the ship. Luckily Lady Ogilvy and her maid were aware of what was about to happen, so when the soldiers appeared on the deck of the ship they were met by her maid who told them that this was no Prince, but merely her mistress who had fallen into debt and was heading abroad to avoid bringing her family into disgrace. When she opened the door of the cabin to show the beautiful Lady Ogilvy sitting at a table in a fancy gown, with her shoulders and upper bosom bare, none of the soldiers had any doubt that this was no man. So she escaped to the Low Countries and headed to France where she was soon reunited with David.

However, Margaret had more adventures yet to come. In 1751 she found out that she was carrying a child. She and David realised that if the son they were hoping for was to have any hope of ever succeeding to his grandfather's estates, it was imperative that he be born in Scotland. So, heavily pregnant, she returned to Scotland in disguise. In her own family's house at Auchterhouse, not far from Dundee, she was delivered of her baby. To everyone's delight it was a boy and a day later his birth was registered by the local minister. Margaret knew that she could not remain in Scotland. If she did it would only be a matter of time before she was arrested and jailed, or worse. So a few weeks later a tearful Lady Ogilvy took farewell of her newborn son to return to France. He was to be brought up by his grandparents, and in time would succeed to the title and lands that were his due, but she realised that she would most likely never see her child again. And it was so, for she died at Boulogne in 1757 without setting eyes on her son, or her native land, again. As for the son she had risked liberty and perhaps life to give birth to in her native land, he grew up severely mentally impaired and never did succeed his grandfather. Her last great adventure had been for nothing.

Bohaldie's Escape

JAMES ROY MCGREGOR of Bohaldie, eldest son of
the infamous Rob Roy, was imprisoned in the
Castle in 1753 after having lost his lands for his
role in the aftermath of the '45. Unlike his father,
Rob Roy McGregor, who had been careful about
declaring his loyalty to one side or another,
Bohaldie – it was common to call Scots by the
lands they owned or leased – had been a major in
the Jacobite Army and had distinguished himself
with his conduct at the Battle of Prestonpans
when the Jacobite Army had routed the British
army under the command of General John Cope.
Such was the extent of that rout that 'Johnny
Cope' is remembered in a humorous song to this
day. However, James was like his father in some
ways and was a man who clung to the old warrior
traditions and raiding ways of the Highland
clans. He had taken an active part in a 'rough
wooing' on behalf of his younger brother Robin
Og McGregor. Rough wooing was something
that had been common throughout Europe in
tribal times and had survived amongst the clan
system of the Scottish Highlands. Basically, it
meant kidnapping a wife. The truth of the matter

is that in many cases it was a pre-arranged set-up where brides were carried off with their full co-operation but was made to look like a raid to conform to ancient traditions.

In this case though, it seems the lass concerned, Jean Kay, a wealthy widow at the tender age of 19, was certainly not informed in advance. The first she knew of Robin Og's intentions was when a group of heavily armed Highlanders arrived at her home in Edinbellie near Balfron. She was taken, bundled up in a plaid and carried off to the hills overlooking Loch Lomond where she was married to Robin. James, it seems, had been the moving spirit behind this outrage and he was arrested and imprisoned in Edinburgh's Tolbooth, or prison. The ancient cateran ways, where the Highlands were under the control of groups of armed clan warriors, had been under attack for centuries but after the slaughter of the Jacobite Army at Culloden in April 1746 and the subsequent suppression of Highland society, there was no way such a throwback could be tolerated by the authorities. Scotland was under an almost total military occupation at the time, and though there were still Jacobites fighting a rearguard, and doomed, guerrilla campaign, there was little chance that James and Robin would be able to get away with this blatant crime. Maybe they thought that Jean Kay would come round to the idea of being married to Robin after a while, but her friends and relations were adamant that the McGregors be brought to justice. So James was captured, taken to Edinburgh in chains, and tried for his part in the abduction. He was duly found guilty and sentenced to death, which, given the government's efforts to control Scotland and suppress any further notions of a Jacobite rising, was hardly surprising. Now James was well known and well liked amongst the Jacobite section of the populace and particularly amongst the dozens of Highlanders who worked as torch-carriers and sedan-chair porters in the capital. He was known to be always ready to buy round after round of drinks for his fellow Highlanders whenever he was in Edinburgh. There were also a few Highlanders amongst the City Guard at this time, and although none of them had been members of the Jacobite forces, the authorities were none too sure of their loyalty. On several occasions over the years, the Tolbooth had been broken open by rioting mobs and the prisoners sprung, thus it was thought prudent to remove

James to the Castle after he had been sentenced. There would be no chance of a rescue from there, or at least, so it was thought. However, the powers that be didn't reckon with the resourcefulness of the McGregor women.

Malie, James eldest daughter, was a strikingly handsome lass, almost as tall as her father, with the same bright red hair that distinguished the family. She and her mother decided to try to effect an escape. So it was that one evening when James' wife had come to visit him in his cell, she and her husband were joined by an old, lame, and apparently hunch-backed cobbler who had come to the Castle gates with a pair of new shoes that had been ordered for the condemned man. The cobbler was dressed in a great black leather apron over a woollen coat with its collar turned up, and a red stocking cap pulled down over his ears, over which he was wearing a broad-brimmed hat. It was November and bitterly cold so no one thought anything of the heavily swaddled figure. Now it was matter of pride amongst Highlanders, particularly those who considered themselves of the chieftain class, to always be well turned out. This ostentation was a noted aspect of clan life and many Highlanders were happy to have little themselves just so their chief could be better dressed than the chiefs of nearby clans. At the very least their chief had to show himself to be every bit as good as other chiefs, which often meant wearing silks and lace while their kinsfolk had only had their plaids, a one piece-tartan garment that could be cleverly folded to provide a kilt below the waist and plenty covering for the upper body too. Generally the clansmen and women wore no shoes and in the depths of winter it was common for warriors out on a raid to soak their plaids in water before sleeping in them outdoors, as wet wool is an even better insulator than dry. Chiefs and chieftains, however, always had to look good. It was deemed particularly important to be seen to cut a bit of a dash if one were to be publicly executed. It was all part of the attitude that led so many Highlanders to be seen as charming and unconcerned right up to the moment of their execution, for they were warriors and what was death to them?

The sentries at the Castle Gate thought it quite normal for a Highlander to behave in this fashion and had let the cobbler through into the castle without even searching him. A short while later the guards outside the cell where James was being held heard an argument break out between Mrs McGregor and the cobbler. Mrs McGregor was complaining bitterly about the quality of the workmanship, and the price, and went on and on. The guards actually felt a little sorry for the poor old cobbler who was being subjected to this tongue-lashing. In truth this harangue was to give time for Malie to slip out of her disguise and allow her father to assume the role of the lame and hunch-backed cobbler. After a while the noise died down and soon after the lame and stooped figure of the cobbler came out of the cell muttering none too quietly about pernickety employers. Slowly he made his way down to the gate and out of the castle, never ceasing to moan about the vagaries of customers who thought they knew better than he, a master craftsman. Once he was out of sight of the guards at the gate, the old cobbler suddenly straightened up, stopped moaning and ran off at speed to a nearby house where friends were waiting. He was quickly guided out of the city through back alleys and vennels to the horse his friends had arranged. Thanking his friends profusely, he mounted the horse and headed off to the coast to board a ship for France. Behind him his daughter simply waited a while till the guards outside the cell changed shift, then walked out of the Castle, smiling prettily to the sentries who did not think to stop this bonny lass. A short while later she was followed by her mother, and it was not until some hours later that it was found that Bohaldie's cell was empty. By then James Roy was long gone, as were his wife and daughter, he to France and they back to the hills. Several of the guards were tried and a couple flogged for allowing this daring escape and the sergeant in charge was reduced to the ranks. As for James Roy, he spent the rest of his long life in France but his brother Robin was not so lucky. He paid the ultimate price for the abduction of Jean Kay, being hanged in the Grassmarket two years later.

prisoners of war

FOR MUCH OF THE time from the start of the American Wars of Independence in 1777 through to 1812, Edinburgh Castle was used as a high-class prisoner of war camp. While there had often been a handful or so of prisoners there in preceding centuries, and a crowd of French prisoners of war in the late 1750s, the castle now became a prison in all but name. Most of the unfortunate inhabitants were sailors captured in sea battles as the British Navy sought to impose itself upon the rebellious American 'colonists' and the European powers who came to their aid. Over the period there were prisoners from America, Denmark, France, Germany, Italy, Poland and even Ireland, showing that the British Empire was ready to fight just about anybody. As had been the case during the years of Jacobite plotting, the European powers were keen to try to bring down the growing British Empire, which was well on the road to being the greatest power on earth. The Americans and the Irish were given a particularly hard time as they were considered to be rebels. In the 1770s and 80s the French, and other nationalities, were given an allowance of up to seven pence a day and a diet that included meat, cheese and even beer, while the rebels were forced to live on just water and one pound of bread a day. On New Year's Day in 1779 the local people actually organised a celebratory feast for the 35 French prisoners who were in the Castle at the time. Not that the others always had it easy.

When the prisoners from the French ship *Marquis de la Fayette* were marched through the city from Leith in 1781, the locals were shocked. The French sailors had just undergone a hellish 14 week journey across the Atlantic, during which time they had been on starvation rations and were little better than skeletons. The people of Edinburgh at once rallied to their assistance, and not long after the last prisoner entered the gates, there were local people arriving with baskets full of vegetables they had dug from their own gardens, while others with cash emptied the bakeries of bread to send to the prisoners. Sadly, despite the best efforts of the capital's citizens, 21 members of the crew died. Captain Le Chevalier de la Neuville, who had been in charge of the *Marquis de la Fayette*, later wrote to the Edinburgh Courant: 'The politeness and humanity which the worthy inhabitants of this city have been pleased to show

me and my cast-away crew, obliges me to return
my most sincere thanks in your paper.' In truth,
the Chevalier had had it a bit easier than his crew.
Like the rest of the officers, being considered
gentlemen they could have parole and not only
be allowed out of the Castle but be permitted to
take lodgings in the city. All they had to do was to
give their word, or parole, not to try and escape.
This was a prerogative denied to the common
sailors, who were treated more like criminals. They
had no such privileges, but for much of the time
their lives do not seem to have been too difficult.
Apart, that is from the problem of boredom.

Many of them used the time that went so
slowly to make things. Using bones from the
meat they were served, some of them carved ships,
others made hats of straw and yet others made
snuff-boxes of bone and scraps of wood, many
of which were beautifully decorated. Carving and
crafting skills had long been common in all
sailing ships, as there were long periods of time
when there was little else to do – so perhaps they
were well prepared for their time on Castle Rock.
This handicraft work was carried out in small
sheds, which had palisades through which they
were permitted to sell their handicrafts to the

locals, who were allowed to visit the Castle between the hours of ten in the morning and half past three in the afternoon. At times the castle must have appeared more like a market place than a prison and was particularly popular amongst the young folk of the city. The prisoners could use this money to buy luxuries such as tobacco. This relaxed atmosphere was a decided bonus for the authorities. Throughout this period, such was the demand for troops to be sent abroad that the Castle was almost entirely staffed by Invalid Pensioner soldiers. These were men who had retired from the army because of injury or old age, and had been re-recruited as prison guards. Luckily they were never really tested. The castle retains a memento or two from those times, among them some interesting graffiti. These are the carved names of three of the inmates, Jean Lefevre, Jean Jacques Ducatez and Peter Garrick. Jean and Jean Jacques were Frenchmen off the captured ship *Rohan Soubise* which had been captured in 1781. On the surviving crew list one of their companions is noted as Pierre Garric. This would seem to be Peter Garrick, who was probably an Irishman, who either passed himself off as one of the crew or had enrolled in the French

Navy to fight the British, something not uncommon for Irishmen up to the 20th century. As long as he was considered to be French he would be entitled to the same rations and allowance as the other prisoners of war. However, if it had been discovered that he was an Irishman and thus a rebel his life would have been a great deal harder, living on bread and water with no way of obtaining money for luxuries, or even necessities.

This was not the only subterfuge that took place amongst the prisoners of war in Edinburgh Castle. In the early years of the 19th century the authorities became aware that the noted skill of the French prisoners of war at carving in bone and wood had developed into something else. A prisoner on a prison ship in England, who had been transferred from Edinburgh, was found to have a Bank of Scotland pound note on his person. Now even a pound was a lot of money to someone who had an allowance of less than a thirtieth of that per day, and there was also some mystery as to how he could have got his hands on a banknote at all. On close inspection it was discovered that the note was in fact a very good forgery. Some of the prisoners had been forging banknotes and circulating these out into the population, with the ready assistance of some of the guards. This was serious indeed and a wholesale search of Edinburgh Castle was ordered. This uncovered a whole set of carved bone stamps created to simulate the die-stamps and watermarks used by the Bank of Scotland. Up to that time bank notes were primarily composed of copperplate handwriting etched into metal which was then used to print the notes. The skill of the French prisoners in copying the penmanship of the notes combined with these excellent examples of carving was a testament to their artistry. No one knew how many such notes had got into circulation and notices were printed in the newspapers warning people to look out for the forgeries. The scare also resulted in much more complicated and pictorial banknotes replacing the older-style ones.

In 1811 a total of 49 French prisoners broke out by tunnelling, and though they were soon captured, it became obvious that the Castle was not really fit to be used as a prison and a new specially built prison was erected at Valleyfield. From then on the number of prisoners kept in the castle began to decline, until at last in 1814 the very last of the French prisoners of war left the Castle on their way to be repatriated. An

eyewitness account of the time described the scene.
The whole town turned out to see the Frenchmen
marching by torchlight, in strict military order all
the way down to the Port of Leith singing their
revolutionary anthems *Ca Ira* and *La Marseillaise*.
The days of the Castle as a prisoner-of-war camp
were over.

a kind-hearted cleric

IN THE PAST CENTURY it has become accepted
under international law that there are certain
humanitarian standards, and that countries
should sign up to treaties that enforce basic
standards of law and imprisonment. Back in the
18th century things were not so clear-cut, and
the very idea of Human Rights was in its infancy.
However, at all times there have been humans
who have answered to their own consciences
despite the laws of the state they lived in. One
such was the Reverend William Fitzsimmons.
Originally from the Isle of Man, he moved to
Scotland in the early 1770s and a few years later
was appointed to the Episcopal Chapel in
Edinburgh. A notable Christian scholar from his
teens, he was well known as a man of considerable
intellect and an upright Christian. In the 1790s
war had broken out between Britain and France
once again, and a group of French prisoners were
locked up in Edinburgh Castle. Just as back in
1781 the local Edinburgh people had rallied
round to help the French prisoners, so there were
people ready to do what they could to help these
unfortunate men. Amongst them was the
Reverend Fitzsimmons who was well known for

having a kind disposition and for helping those less fortunate than himself. He simply saw it as his Christian duty. His visits to the prisoners with food and blankets were greatly appreciated by the Frenchmen, as being locked up in the filthy cells hewn out of the Castle Rock was no picnic. This was well before any ideas of prison reform came into fashion and it wasn't just prisoners of war who suffered.

Those who could afford to have their food, drink, and even fuel brought in to their cells could at least eat and be warm, but like their poorer and even more miserable companions, all fought a constant battle with dirt and disease. The conditions in the Castle dungeons turned Fitzsimmon's stomach but there was little he or anyone else could do. Some of the Frenchmen, however, were set on helping themselves. Spurred on, no doubt, by stories of previous escapes, a couple of the bolder soldiers decided to break out of their prison. They decided that if they managed to get away from the Castle they would go and throw themselves on the mercy of the Reverend Fitzsimmons, of whom they had heard so much, but whom they had never directly met. They had been fortunate in that a sword blade had been smuggled in to them by a local clerk who was one of many people in Scotland who saw the Revolution in France as a positive development. Scotland was at the time under the rigid and utterly corrupt control of Lord Henry Dundas, known to enemies and friends alike as Henry the 9th, due to the extent of the power he had over Scotland under the Westminster Parliament. Show trials of men calling for democratic reform had taken place a few years earlier, the most famous of them being Thomas Muir, the only man ever to escape back to Europe from Botany Bay, and who himself became a hero of the French Revolution after a journey round the world.

It seems unlikely that William Fitzsimmons had much direct sympathy for the Revolutionary cause, he was after all an Episcopalian minister and public opinion had swung against the French Revolution after an initial strong level of support, occasioned by the awareness that France was a country controlled by a corrupt system. The fate of Muir and others suggested that the much vaunted British state was only marginally less repressive than the *Ancien Regime* of the French monarchs had been. Certainly, under the iron fist of Dundas, Scotland was kept on a tight leash.

It was a cold and windy night in March of 1799 that the two Frenchmen made their move. They had been chipping and sawing away at the bars of their cell for a couple of weeks and at last had managed to get themselves free. It was a Sunday night. Having spied out the lay of the castle on the few occasions they were allowed outside, they managed to make their way to the gate. Security was pretty lax, perhaps because it was the Sabbath, and under cover of darkness they managed to slip out of the castle. They were dressed in distinctive prison uniforms of a yellow colour, but as the night was so cold there were few people in the streets, and those who were hurried along, allowing the two prisoners to make their way unchallenged through the streets to Fitzsimmons' house. At about 10.30 they knocked on the door, which was opened by a maid, and asked to speak to the Reverend Fitzsimmons. Although taken aback at the dirty and ill-dressed foreigners the maid went and informed William that two men had come to call, leaving them standing in the hall. At once Fitzsimmons, and his nephew John Quillin who was staying with him, came out to see who was there. Although he did not recognise either of the two men William immediately knew who they were. His decision was instantaneous, there was no way he would allow these unfortunates to go back to their filthy cell. He would help them. The two men were given food and drink, and after swearing his maid to secrecy, Fitzsimmons gave up his bed to the Frenchmen. During the night they were awakened by one of the Frenchmen crying like a child, whether in relief or because of some deep trauma it is impossible to say.

The following day they arranged for new clothes for the Frenchmen, who were delighted to have the chance to clean themselves up at last. Meanwhile Fitzsimmons went out to surreptitiously sound out the possibility of getting the Frenchmen out of Scotland. He was well enough aware that what he was doing was treason, but he just could not face the idea of turning the men in to return to their miserable existence in the castle. There were still enough people sympathetic to the French cause for finding help to be relatively straight-forward, and within a day or two he had arranged for the men to be taken out later in the week from the Port of Leith to a fishing boat, anchored off the island of Inchkeith. The captain of the ship was prepared, for a price, to take the prisoners and

land them somewhere safe on the Continental
mainland, from where they could return to their
homes. While all this was being set up, however,
a further development occurred. On the Monday
night there was another knock at Fitzsimmons'
door. This time he answered it himself. Two more
French prisoners stood there. This pair had been
given parole, which meant that they had been
allowed to leave the Castle having given their
word to return, and had simply not gone back to
the Castle at the designated time. Clearly the escape
of their two companions had not yet been noticed.
These two Frenchmen were given beds on a shake
down on the floor of the minister's sitting room.

The next four days were fraught with tension.
It was a small house and the six men made it a
bit crowded. To prevent any suspicion Fitzsimmons
and Quillin dined out three of the four nights,
acting as if everything was just as normal. By the
Wednesday the escapes were common knowledge
but it appeared, luckily for Fitzsimmons, that the
Commander of the Castle had decided that the
Frenchmen were already well away from the
capital, and security, though increased, was
hardly a real problem for Fitzsimmons and his
unforeseen guests. So it was that at four in the

morning on Friday, Fitzsimmons and the four disguised Frenchmen travelled through the back streets of Edinburgh and down through open country to the port at Leith. Here they were put in a small boat and ferried out to Inchkeith where they were to be picked up later. We can imagine just how thankful the Frenchmen were to their benefactor. All seemed well, and Fitzsimmons and Quillin were sure that their kind-hearted, if ultimately treasonous, actions would not be discovered. The fishing boat sailed out into the North Sea, landed the Frenchmen somewhere in the Netherlands and returned to the open sea to look for a catch.

It was not until they returned to Leith that problems arose. One of the fishermen, after a few drinks, had let slip that his boat had ferried the prisoners to the Continent and it was just matter of time before he was arrested and things began to escalate. The role of Fitzsimmons and his nephew was soon known and they were arrested and charged with helping enemies of the state to escape. The charges against Quillin were soon dropped as it was thought that he had been under the influence of the older man, and though there was lot of local sympathy for Fitzsimmons

it was all too obvious that the charges against
him were extremely serious. The ultimate penalty
for treason was death. Much of the population
of Edinburgh were sympathetic to the pickle
Fitzsimmons found himself in, and he had the
extreme good fortune to secure the services of his
friend, The Honourable Henry Erskine, to defend
him. Erskine was one of the most famous
advocates of his time and was well used to
appearing before the High Court of Justiciary
where William was to be tried. He was also very
much a member of the Establishment, having
already been Lord Advocate, a position he again
held a decade after the trial. He had been the
Dean of the Faculty of Advocates for ten years
up to 1795 but his resistance to the new laws
against sedition and treason that had been
pushed through the Westminster Parliament as a
knee-jerk reaction against the French Revolution,
made working for the current administration
impossible. In defending Fitzsimmons he could
show his contempt for what he saw as
government high-handedness.

His defence was basically that Fitzsimmons,
though technically guilty, had been motivated by
the most honourable of intentions. He told the

court that, 'Whoever may hear of this trial will only hear that the unhappy man at the bar stands accused of the virtue of humanity and the error of rashness.' To bolster this defence he called a series of character witnesses, including high-ranking serving army officers, all of whom stressed that though William had indeed been rash, he had been motivated by nothing more than Christian kindness. This presentation of support from members of Edinburgh's great and good was followed by a remarkable statement. The prosecution of such a serious crime in the highest court of the land had been led by the country's top legal officer, the Lord Advocate. In his closing speech he too spoke extensively of the accused's Christian virtue and common humanity. However, there was no chance of William being found not guilty and he knew it. The jury duly delivered a guilty verdict but they recommended that the punishment should be as lenient as was possible. So it was that William Fitzsimmons, found guilty of helping foreign prisoners to escape from Edinburgh Castle, was sentenced to three months to be served in Edinburgh's Tolbooth prison. His supporters had done him proud. For committing an act that was clearly treasonous he had received little more than a slap on the wrist.

A few years earlier James Mealmaker, a weaver from Dunfermline, had been sentenced to lifelong transportation to Botany Bay for simply handing out copies of Thomas Paine's book *The Rights of Man*. It has long been said that in Edinburgh it's not what you know but who you know that matters, and having friends in high places certainly worked for William. After serving his sentence he felt he had had enough of public exposure and returned to his native Isle of Man where he led the life of a country landowner, devoting his time to his small estate, much more interested in growing trees than the affairs of state. He had become entangled with the law often enough for one lifetime.

the scottish regalia and the wizard of the north

SIR WALTER SCOTT was a remarkable man. While practising as a lawyer in his mid-twenties, he took to writing. He drew upon his deep interest in Scottish history and culture to bring out *The Minstrelsy of the Scottish Border*, a three-volume collection of ballads and poems from his native Borders area. In 1805 he went on to achieve worldwide fame with the publication of his first collection of poetry, *The Lay of the Last Minstrel*, which also drew on his interest in Scotland's past. However, it was as a novelist that he is best remembered. His first novel *Waverley*, published in 1814, was written to raise much-needed cash. Due to an over-commitment to publishing he was in substantial debt and over the next few years as his popularity grew throughout the English-speaking world his output was prodigious. Many of his early novels were based on Scottish history, even if it now appears a peculiarly romanticised vision of Scotland's past, and there is no doubt that he was the first truly great historical novelist. His works are still read today and are still accepted as of major importance to the development of Scottish and English Literature.

The great American writer Mark Twain even went so far as to blame Sir Walter Scott for the American Civil War. Twain reckoned that the gentlemen of the south were raised on Scott's romantic ideas of fighting for a noble cause and thus went into wars against superior forces that they could never win. Scott's interest in the history of his native land was deep and sincere. In 1818, having been researching the period around the Treaty of Union, he became aware that the Crown and Regalia of Scotland had not been seen since those troubled times. He therefore decided to try to find them. The Honours of Scotland, as they are also known, consist of the Crown, the Sceptre and the Sword of State. The Crown dates from before 1540, when it was remodelled for the coronation of James V, the Sword, a gift from the Pope, dates from 1507, and the Sceptre is even older. The Honours were first used together in 1543 at the bizarre coronation ceremony of the 9-month old Mary, Queen of Scots. While their value as both precious items and historical artefacts is considerable, to Sir Walter they had another, and deeper significance.

The Honours were last used in 1650 when Charles II was crowned King of Scots at Scone, after the English Parliamentarians under Cromwell had beheaded his father, Charles I, on 30 January 1649, and abolished the monarchy in England at a stroke. Cromwell arrived in Scotland from Ireland not long after, and though, due to his sympathy with Scottish Presbyterianism, his Scottish campaign was not as brutal as the one against the Catholics in Ireland had been, if things were not as bad in Scotland, they were bad enough. By a stroke of good fortune he had been victorious at the Battle of Dunbar on 3 September, just when he was on the point of retreating from Scotland. From then on his luck changed and soon he had subdued most of the country. After the Battle of Dunbar, the Scots opposed to him received intelligence that the Lord Protector, as he styled himself, was set on getting his hands on the Honours of Scotland. It seems he had been led to believe that they were items of much greater value than they truly were. They were of course of great significance to the Scots, regardless of their monetary value. They were a symbol of the country's independence and what we would nowadays call national identity. So they were sent off to be stored in Dunottar Castle, a massive and awe-inspiring fortress on the east coast, south of Aberdeen. However Cromwell soon found out where they were and a force was sent to lay siege to Dunottar to get the jewels.

Ogilvy of Barras was in command of the great fortress and knew well that, even with his cannons and the new model army he had created, Cromwell would be very lucky to break his way into the massive castle. However, isolated on a spit of land as it is, Dunottar always had one weakness. As long as a besieging army had the patience to wait, and could stop ships supplying the defenders from the sea, the garrison could be starved out. Once the English army had arrived and isolated the castle, Ogilvy needed a plan. He discussed the matter with the Reverend Dr Grainger, minister at nearby Kineff and like many clergymen of the time, heavily involved in the ongoing battle against the English Parliamentarian Army. Grainger thought that they should include his wife in the discussions, having a high regard for her intellect. And so a plan was formed. First a rumour was started that the Honours had been sent to the

Continent to keep them safe. Now Mr and Mrs
Grainger had safe conduct through to the castle
and she asked if she could remove several bundles
of lint that she owned and claimed she needed.
She explained to the English commander that
times were hard and they needed money to feed
their children. The lint was hers and she wanted
to sell it. Her ploy worked and she was given
leave to bring out a handcart with the bundles of
lint. It must have been an exciting episode for her
as she left the great walls of the castle, pushing
her handcart in which the Honours of Scotland
were well hidden. Once she was back home she
and her husband waited till the dead of night,
and then sneaked out to the church. Here they
buried the jewels under the floorboards at the
bottom of the pulpit. Months later when the
castle at last surrendered, there was uproar, where
were the jewels? Threats and even torture gave
up no more information than that most people
thought they were long gone to the Continent.
The English Army had to leave empty-handed.

A few years later, in 1660, Charles II was
restored to the crowns of both Scotland and
England and the Honours were returned with all
ceremony to Edinburgh by Ogilvy. He and his

son were both rewarded and honoured but the Graingers, for all their loyalty and commitment, as Sir Walter Scott himself wrote, they got 'the hare's foot to lick'. That is, absolutely nothing. Their central role in the saving of the Regalia was ignored. Charles did not last that long as monarch and was himself deposed in 1688.

Tensions between Scotland and England remained high into 1707 as the Treaty of Union became imminent. Rumours flashed around Edinburgh that the Honours of Scotland were to be removed to London. Given that the Union was forced through, and that the vast majority of the Scottish people were strongly against unification with the ancient enemy, such a move would have been dangerous. The people of Edinburgh were always ready to riot and in the tense period leading up to the signing of the Treaty of Union, such a riot could have sparked off trouble throughout the whole country. It was therefore explicitly stated in the Act of Union that the Honours of Scotland were to remain in the country for all time, which in government terms probably had the sub-text, till they could be safely moved. In a solemn ceremony, representatives of the Three Estates who made up the Scottish Parliament watched as the Crown, the Sceptre and the Sword of State were ceremoniously locked up in the great black kist, or chest, that they are still housed in.

Over the ensuing years there was much to think about as the Union began to take hold and in time the Honours were forgotten about. Until Walter Scott took an interest. He was fascinated by the idea that these ancient symbols of Scottish nationhood were still somewhere within the Castle. Now Scott was both a Unionist and a proud Scot, and in 1817 he petitioned the Prince Regent, later King George iv, to search for them. The Regent was already an admirer of Scott's, going so far as to make him a baronet a couple of years later, so was happy to oblige. He therefore set up a Commission to locate the Scottish Honours under the guidance of Scott. So it was that one day, with a goldsmith and a couple of soldiers, Scott and the Governor of the Castle broke into the room in the bowels of the castle that had been locked since 1707. There, in the bottom of the black kist, wrapped in linen, were the Honours of Scotland. This is how he described it in a letter to a friend:

> The extreme solemnity of opening sealed
> doors of oak and iron, and finally breaking

open a chest which had been shut since
7th March 1707, about a hundred and
eleven years, gave a sort of interest to our
researches, which I can hardly express to
you, and it would be very difficult to
describe the intense eagerness with which
we watched the rising of the lid of the
chest, and the progress of the workmen in
breaking it open, which was neither an
easy nor a speedy task. It sounded very
hollow when they worked on it with their
tools, and I began to lean to your faction
of the Little Faiths. However, I never could
assign any probable or feasible reason for
withdrawing these memorials of ancient
independence; and my doubts rather arose
from the conviction that many absurd
things are done in public as well as in
private life, merely out of a hasty
impression of passion or resentment. For
it was evident the removal of the Regalia
might have greatly irritated people's
minds here, and offered a fair pretext of
breaking the Union, which for thirty
years was the predominant wish of the
Scottish nation.

Scott was delighted to have located the Regalia and within days they were put on display and they have been open to public view ever since.

the Return of an auld stane

ON ST ANDREW'S DAY in 1996 a solemn ceremonial took place at Edinburgh Castle. With about ten thousand spectators lining the Royal Mile from Holyrood Palace up to the Castle, a Land Rover drove slowly up the cobbled street. It was escorted by kilted soldiers and preceded by a piper. Following the lead vehicle were a crowd of dignitaries, led by Prince Andrew, representing his mother, the Queen. This stately occasion was the ceremonial return of the fabled Stone of Destiny, upon which Scottish kings were said to have been crowned in the Early Medieval Period. Arriving at the Castle the Prince handed the stone over to the then Secretary of State for Scotland, Michael Forsyth, a member of the Conservative government. Inside the early-16th-century Great Hall of the Castle, the block of red sandstone was laid on a velvet cloth on an oak table before the grand fireplace.

Supposedly dating from the far distant past, the Stone of Scone, as it is sometimes called, had been stolen by the English King Edward I from

Scone Abbey, just north of Perth, during his unsuccessful attempt to conquer Scotland in 1296. He intended having himself crowned King of Scots on the stone once he had subdued the natives. This he hoped would legitimise his conquest and fulfil his ambition of ruling the whole of Britain. Tellingly, the bronze throne he ordered to be built to house the stone was never made, he cancelled it soon after. Perhaps he had realised that the stone might not be the real one. Anyway he never did manage to conquer the Scots, just like all the other English kings who tried, and before them, the Romans and Vikings. And Robert the Bruce, King of Scots at the time, never seems to have made any effort at all to reclaim such an important, and vital, national treasure.

Variously described as the Stone of Destiny or the Stone of Scone, the Marble Chair, or even the Lia Fail, this artifact has been the focus of many legends down the centuries. Some tales say that it was the stone that Joseph laid his head upon when he watched the angels ascend to heaven in the story from the Christian Bible. According to another version the stone came to Scotland with Scota, daughter of an Egyptian Pharaoh, via the Iberian peninsula and Ireland.

Another version claims it to be the semi-mythical Lia Fail, the roaring stone, originally from Ireland, which let out a mighty bellow whenever the rightful king sat upon it. Others claimed it to have originally been a Roman altar stone and yet another theory suggests it may have been a meteorite.

In a religious ceremony to mark the event, the Moderator of the Church of Scotland, the Right Reverend John McIndoe, declared that the return of the stone would, 'strengthen the proud distinctiveness of the people of Scotland'. At the Castle, once the stone had been placed in its new room, a 21 gun salute was fired from the Half-Moon Battery. Out in the sea road of the Firth of Forth, under the clear blue November skies, an answering salute came from *The HMS Newcastle*, lying anchored off Leith harbour. However, apart from the invited congregation in St Giles, a great number of the crowds watching the return of this ancient national treasure that November day were tourists. Many others were children brought in by bus from surrounding schools. The native Scots stayed away in droves. Why? Surely this was a day to celebrate – Scotland's ancient coronation stone had been restored to the ancient capital of the country after 700 years. Surely this ceremony would make up for the fact that it had been taken in the first place? This was surely a treasure to match the Scottish Regalia – the oldest crown jewels in Europe – which are kept in the Castle.

Perhaps the people who stayed away in their droves knew of the story from Perthshire, which said that the Abbot of Scone, on hearing of the approach of the English army, had loaded the ancient relic on to a cart and then took it off to the east and buried it on Dunsinane Hill, made famous in Shakespeare's play *Macbeth*. A large black stone was found there in a 19th century excavation, accompanied by a bronze plaque claiming it to be the original stone, but the records are vague and the plaque has not survived. Others perhaps were aware of the events surrounding the theft of the stone on Christmas Day 1950. This was a stunt pulled off by nationalist students who had simply gone into Westminster Abbey one night and lifted it. They then brought it back to Scotland, risking imprisonment as they dodged the road blocks. For months there was uproar as the police tried to locate the famous stone, and in between the theft and its eventual return on the altar at Arbroath Abbey on 11 April 1951, several copies are believed to have been made. What is indisputable is that part of it broke off during its acquisition that Christmas, and the repair needed the services of a professional stonemason. Many people think that if the stone from Westminster Abbey was originally a forgery, then the one that went back was a forgery of a forgery. The stone taken by Iain Hamilton, Gavin Vernon, Kay Matheson and Alan Stuart in 1950 is now thought to be hidden in a Perthshire glen. Whatever the real story, one thing is clear. A great many people in Scotland doubt there is much to the lump of red sandstone currently so well defended in Edinburgh Castle. After all, virtually all of Perthshire is made of red sandstone.

the last prisoner

THROUGHOUT THE CENTURIES Edinburgh Castle has been associated with many of Scotland's kings and queens and has served as prison for many aristocratic inmates. Some of them, like Lady Ogilvy, were noted for their heroism while others, like the 7th Earl of Kellie, had a different kind of reputation. Like Lady Ogilvy, The Earl of Kellie was locked up in the castle after the Jacobite rebellion of 1745. He was as popular with his co-prisoners as he was with the tenants on his estate in Fife, and for the same reason. He was a lover of conviviality, which is another way of saying he liked a good drink, and his great love was the fiddle. He was in fact known throughout much of Scotland as Fiddler Tam, rather than by his title, and was happy to play music, and drink, with the humblest shepherd or boatman as any of his aristocratic peers. However, probably the strangest of all the Lords to have passed time in the cells of Edinburgh Castle was its last ever prisoner.

During World War 1, the workers of the Clydeside shipyard in Glasgow had a reputation for radicalism. The revolution in Russia had struck a chord with many of them who were strongly opposed to the capitalist system where the rich and powerful ruled the roost. Despite the ongoing war with Germany the Clydesiders formed the Clyde Workers Committee with the express intention of agitating for widespread reform. In the eyes of the British Government this was a potentially seditious organisation, a view that had been strengthened by the strike for better pay that had stopped the shipyards in 1915. The fact that a great many of Glasgow shipyard workers opposed the war against Germany on the grounds that it was just a capitalist squabble certainly didn't help. One of the leading members of the CWC was David Kirkwood, a shop steward at the Parkhead Forge. Along with John Maclean who was appointed by the Russian leader, Lenin, to be the ambassador of the Soviet Government in Britain, and Willie Gallacher, who went on to be a Communist MP in the House of Commons, Kirkwood was a thorn in the flesh of the Ministry of Munitions. The Ministry constantly used the excuse of the war to dilute the pay and conditions of the workers, and time and again Kirkwood opposed them, pointing out that while they were attacking the workers' conditions they were not attempting to limit the profits being made by the shipyard owners. The situation became so severe that the Minister of Munitions, David Lloyd George, made a personal visit to Clydeside to address the ship workers. He was booed by many of the crowd who then united in singing the Red Flag as a token of their resistance. However, negotiations between owners and workers were re-opened and things quietened down for a while.

Unrest flared again in 1916 and of course Davie Kirkwood was in the thick of it. This time the government moved quickly. A group of detectives arrived at Kirkwood's door one morning at 3am and arrested him. Along with a bunch of his comrades he was then taken to Edinburgh and told to keep out of Glasgow. The irony of the British Government trying to impose internal exile, which had no legal standing, because of their fear of the Soviet Union is striking. In the Soviet Union internal exile became one of the most widely used tools of repression. However, because there was no real legal sanction for this activity, it was only a matter of days before Davie and his friends returned to Glasgow and re-entered the fray. This time, however, the police were ready for him and when they arrested him and took him through to the capital, they did not turn him loose on Princes Street but marched him up to the High Street and threw him into one of the old cells deep in the bowels of the Castle.

His fellow agitator John Maclean was locked up in the Calton Jail on nearby Calton Hill. Some of the War Cabinet realised that as long as he was locked up Kirkwood, like John Maclean, could be made to look like a martyr to his workmates. Therefore it was only a matter of months before Winston Churchill prevailed upon Lloyd George and the rest of the Cabinet to set Red Davie free. This had the desired effect and till the end of the war the Clydeside workforce knuckled down and supported the war effort, Kirkwood himself taking pride in the increased output and efficiency of the shipyards in this period.

However, once the war was over, there were still many grievances outstanding and in 1919 Davie was again to the fore in another strike. The government sent in troops to Glasgow in what is known as 'Black Friday', and Davie Kirkwood ended up in hospital having been knocked unconscious by a police truncheon. However, times were changing in the aftermath of the war and Davie decided to stand as a Parliamentary candidate for the Labour Party. In 1922 he was elected MP for Dunbartonshire and continued to represent the constituency till 1951. He then retired and soon found himself being offered a peerage for his services to Parliament. He then entered the House of Lords as Baron Kirkwood of Bearsden. Unlike Gallacher and Maclean, Kirkwood was never a Communist and there were those who reckoned he sold out in accepting a peerage. Whatever the truth of that there is little doubt that he came a long way from being the son of a labourer in Glasgow's impoverished East End, from an imprisoned agitator to a member of the British House of Lords, and his story is truly unique. He eventually died in 1955 at the age of 82 with the noted distinciton not only of having risen to the peerage but having been the very last prisoner to be held in Edinburgh Castle.

Some other books published by **LUATH** PRESS

Luath Storyteller: Tales of the Picts

Stuart McHardy

ISBN 1 84282 097 4 PBK £5.99

For many centuries the people of Scotland have told stories of their ancestors, a mysterious tribe called the Picts. This ancient Celtic-speaking people, who fought off the might of the Roman Empire, are perhaps best known for their Symbol Stones – images carved into standing stones left scattered across Scotland, many of which have their own stories. Here for the first time these tales are gathered together with folk memories of bloody battles, chronicles of warriors and priestesses, saints and supernatural beings. From Shetland to the Border with England, these ancient memories of Scotland's original inhabitants have flourished since the nation's earliest days and now are told afresh, shedding new light on our ancient past.

Luath Storyteller: Highland Myths & Legends

George W Macpherson

ISBN 1 84282 064 8 PBK £5.99

The mythical, the legendary, the true – this is the stuff of stories and storytellers, the preserve of Scotland's ancient oral tradition.

Celtic heroes, fairies, Druids, selkies, sea horses, magicians, giants, Viking invaders – all feature in this collection of traditional Scottish tales, the like of which have been told around campfires for centuries and are still told today.

Drawn from storyteller George W Macpherson's extraordinary repertoire of tales and lore, each story has been passed down through generations of oral tradition – some are over 2,500 years old. Strands of these timeless tales cross over and interweave to create a delicate tapestry of Highland Scotland as depicted by its myths and legends.

I have heard George telling his stories... and it is an unforgettable experience... This is a unique book and a 'must buy'...

DALRIADA: THE JOURNAL OF CELTIC HERITAGE AND CULTURAL TRADITIONS

On the Trail of the Holy Grail

Stuart McHardy
ISBN 1 905222 53 X PBK £7.99

New theories appear and old ideas are re-configured as this remarkable story continues to fascinate and enthral.

Scholars have long known that the Grail is essentially legendary, a mystic symbol forever sought by those seeking Enlightenment, a quest in which the search is as important as the result. Time and again it has been said that the Grail is a construct of mystical Christian ideas and motifs from the ancient oral tradition of the Celtic-speaking peoples of Britain. There is much to commend this view, but now, drawing on decades of research in his native Scotland, in a major new contribution to the Grail legend, the field historian and folklorist Stuart McHardy traces the origin of the idea of fertility and regeneration back beyond the time of the Celtic warrior tribes of Britain to a truly ancient, physical source.

A physical source as dynamic and awesome today as it was in prehistory when humans first encountered it and began to weave the myths that grew into the Legend of the Holy Grail.

...a refreshingly different approach to the origin of the Grail.
NORTHERN EARTH

On the Trail of Scotland's Myths and Legends

Stuart McHardy
ISBN 1 84282 049 4 PBK £7.99

A journey through Scotland's past from the earliest times through the medium of the awe-inspiring stories that were at the heart our ancestors' traditions and beliefs.

As the art of storytelling bursts into new flower, many tales are being told again as they once were. As *On the Trail of Scotland's Myths and Legends* unfolds, mythical animals, supernatural beings, heroes, giants and goddesses come alive and walk Scotland's rich landscape as they did in the time of the Scots, Gaelic and Norse speakers of the past.

Visiting over 170 sites across Scotland, Stuart McHardy traces the lore of our ancestors, connecting ancient beliefs with traditions still alive today. Presenting a new picture of who the Scots are and where they have come from, this book provides an insight into a unique tradition of myth, legend and folklore that has marked the language and landscape of Scotland.

This is a revised and updated edition of Stuart McHardy's popular *Highland Myths and Legends*.

This remains an entertaining record of the extent to which history is memorialised in the landscape.
THE SCOTSMAN

Luath Press Limited

committed to publishing well written books worth reading

LUATH PRESS takes its name from Robert Burns, whose little collie Luath (*Gael.*, swift or nimble) tripped up Jean Armour at a wedding and gave him the chance to speak to the woman who was to be his wife and the abiding love of his life. Burns called one of 'The Twa Dogs' Luath after Cuchullin's hunting dog in Ossian's *Fingal*. Luath Press was established in 1981 in the heart of Burns country, and now resides a few steps up the road from Burns' first lodgings on Edinburgh's Royal Mile.

Luath offers you distinctive writing with a hint of unexpected pleasures.

Most bookshops in the UK, the US, Canada, Australia, New Zealand and parts of Europe either carry our books in stock or can order them for you. To order direct from us, please send a £sterling cheque, postal order, international money order or your credit card details (number, address of cardholder and expiry date) to us at the address below. Please add post and packing as follows: UK – £1.00 per delivery address; overseas surface mail – £2.50 per delivery address; overseas airmail – £3.50 for the first book to each delivery address, plus £1.00 for each additional book by airmail to the same address. If your order is a gift, we will happily enclose your card or message at no extra charge.

Luath Press Limited
543/2 Castlehill
The Royal Mile
Edinburgh EH1 2ND
Scotland

Telephone: 0131 225 4326 (24 hours)
email: sales@luath.co.uk
Website: www.luath.co.uk